I0452120

The Apple Man's Stories: Volume II
A Compilation of Short Stories
By Paul McAllister

ISBN: 978-1-926977-29-4

The Apple Man's Stories Vol II

By Paul McAllister

Contents

ACKNOWLEDGEMENTS

I wish to thank my brother-in-law, John Astle, who translated my handwriting and put it in type. I have to also thank my wife, Sylvia, for forgiving my "absence of mind" as I was off in my other "adventures".

After writing my first book, I would like to thank my fellow writers and friends for encouraging me to continue. Since I had a treasure trove of stories to tell, I have continued my tales on in Volume II. I hope you find it as enjoyable as my first.

Some stories are true.

Some are not.

You can judge them yourself.

Names have been changed in some stories.

ALASKA FISHING TRIP

A couple of years ago my friend Tony said he would like to go to Alaska. I said I thought that would be a lovely trip. "Then why don't you and Mary come with us?"

"Yes," said his wife Sue, "why don't you?" We would love to have you along; there is lots of room in our motor home for four people."

"Well, er... ah... I would love to but I don't know." I couldn't say yes until I talked it over with Mary. It would cost quite a bit and Mary was still working, but she was talking about retiring soon.

"When are you planning on going?" Mary asked Sue.

"Tony would like to go next year in the early summer so he can be back home in time to do haying. Would that be alright with you?" she asked.

I was surprised to hear her say yes she would love to go; besides she would be retired by then.

"Settled then," said Sue, "we will plan on going next year. We will have lots of time to get ready."

The waiter at "the Keg" came and re-filled our glasses and we raised them in unison to Alaska. A few days later we said good-by to our Alberta friends in Grande Prairie and flew back to New Brunswick.

Surprising how fast the winter went by as we read everything we could find about Alaska. By mid May we were back in Grande Prairie again as Mary wanted to spend a few days with our daughter and son-in-law and of course our grandson, before departing on our trip.

As planned we left on May the twenty-second. "You sit in front there with Tony, Tom," says Sue. "Mary and I will sit back here on the chesterfield and talk." That was alright by me; Tony and I could talk about things that didn't interest them anyway. They would be quite comfortable back there in their living room atmosphere looking out through the big picture windows on the sides of the motor home.

Tony did the driving; I tried to get everything interesting on video. I got lots of shots of the white-capped mountains and the deep valleys below. It was a beautiful drive as the wildflowers of all colours were in blossom on the sides of the road. We saw quite a few wild animals, moose, deer, a wild buffalo and some mountain goats. The black bears were feasting on the dandelions and didn't pay any attention to the photographers zooming in on them.

After five days we came to Dawson City. We noticed quite a change in the landscape as we drove in on a flat plain beside the Yukon River. Gravel, or rather beach stone, was piled up in uneven cones on both sides of the road. We were to learn that dredges as large as a three story building dug their own path as they sifted through the gravel beds searching for gold nuggets. There wasn't much concern for the environment back at the turn of the twentieth century. Dawson City is preserved just as it was in the gold rush of 1898 to 1902. This makes it a great tourist attraction.

The Yukon is called the land of the mid-night sun as we were about to find out. We went to see a floor show at Gold Tooth Gertie's Casino. Half a dozen young beautiful girls danced waving their frilly dresses. They were kicking up their legs and bending over showing their bottoms as the musicians played their honky-tonk tunes. We all enjoyed the show especially Tony and I.

When we left around one in the morning the sun was still up, almost, in the North and it was bright enough to read a newspaper. People were milling around town the same as they do in the early evening back home.

Dawson boasts Canada's most northern golf course. Our second night there Tony and I started our game at eight o'clock. When we finished at eleven it was still as bright as when we started. We learned they had hosted a men's tournament in nineteen ninety-eight at midnight. This was in connection with their centennial celebration since the start of the gold rush. While we were at the "Top of the World" golf course, as it was called, a helicopter landed in the far side of the parking lot. Two young men jumped out with their golf bags. Apparently there was still a few small family mining operations going on. Some are doing quite good at it but the environmental people are giving them a hard time.

Of course I had to go to see the Robert Service cabin on the edge of town. Jack London and Pierre Berton's old homes were also in the same area.

Since we didn't want to return on the same road we came up on we decided to make a large round turn down to the interior of British Columbia. We calculated we had enough time to take in a little fishing at Steward, British Columbia. There is a one hundred mile fjord there that separates Alaska and Canada. Alaska is on the North and British Columbia has the South side, the border is fair in the middle. The trees were large in this area, probably a couple hundred feet tall and up to six feet in diameter.

We found an outfitter who would take us out for the day. He supplied everything, boat and tackle and acted as out private guide. He said he would give us a deal for five hundred. We also had to buy a one day license for twenty-five each. We split the cost and were to start at eight next morning.

There was a rodeo going on in town that day so our women opted to take that in. They joked as we left that they would "have the frying pan hot" when we returned. We were impressed with his twenty-five foot all aluminum diesel. It was a modern boat with a nice cabin; it had a depth finder and a fish finder, along with a G.P.S. System and all the safety equipment.

As we sailed ten miles down the fjord to better fishing grounds we discovered that our guide was a great story teller. He told us that being an outfitter was a lonely life; he was out on the water nearly every day in summer. When he wasn't guiding; he was a beachcomber picking up stray logs that had escaped out of a log boom. He said his third wife would turn off the C.B radio when he went out, but he added he liked the one he has now. She would clean fish or do anything she could to help him.

When we reached the fishing ground our guide Ron MacFazden showed me how to bait our hook with a fresh sardine. Then he ran our lines through a loop in ten pound sinkers. This was to keep lines down at seventy-five and eighty-five feet as we trolled quite close to shore at three miles per hour. Tony had a strike right away but it got free after a minute. He replaced his bait and at ten o'clock he was lucky again. After a ten minute fight he landed a thirty-five pound salmon. I got the whole thing on Video but I had to set the camera down in order to help Ron lift the scoop net onto the boat.

We were in a happy mood now and dipped into the cooler quite frequently. At least we wouldn't be skunked; the women wouldn't be able to chide us now. We set our rods in the holders so we could keep an eye on them as we played around with our Video cameras. The scenery was beautiful; the white capped mountains came right down into the water. Mr. MacFazden said that in some places there was one thousand feet of water.

I tried focusing in on a soaring eagle and some jet passenger planes as they headed west. Where were they going I wonder, west of British Columbia, would that be Russia? We never even got a strike all afternoon as we trolled along. We decided we would reel in at four o'clock and head back to the wharf. At ten to four I noticed my rod starting to twitch. "I think I hooked one," I reported, as I picked up my rod.

"Hold a tight line," Ron warned, "but not too tight, let him run a little." He reeled up the weight sinker up so he would be easier to play at the surface. At one time I must have had four hundred feet of line out. Then the salmon turned and headed for our boat. I had to reel fast in order to keep the line taunt. In British Columbia we weren't allowed to fish with a barbed hook. I knew this was my last chance so I did my best. The salmon turned away a couple of times but after ten minutes I was able to work him up to the waiting scoop net.

My salmon was five pounds lighter than Tony's but I was happy to settle for that. When we stopped at our campground to show off our fish our women were amazed at out luck to say the least. Ron took the salmon to his place and filleted them for us. We shook hands with our new found friend and promised we would come back again some time.

BRYENTON SIDING

Driving through the sleepy little community of Bryenton one might think it looked like this forever. Ask anyone who lived there all their life and they will recall quite a transformation. For better or worse, everyone has their translation. Of course the days of my youth leave the best memories.

As I sit here in my old lazy-boy chair in comfortable surroundings I reflect on the old days. Two young lads, my brother David and I; racing our bicycles. "Race you to the siding," and off we go. Up the road to Bryenton's General Store, then back the lane to the siding. We get there at the same time to join the half dozen bicycles already lying on the grass beside the loading platform. We can hear lots of jeering going on inside. Gerald has just done twelve chin-ups and Bev is up to nine when we join in. They are the big boys and our mentors.

I remember Bev with fondness; he saved my life I believe. That was one summer while we were all at the river for a little swim. I was out over my head and couldn't swim. Of course the order of the day was that the older children were responsible for the younger ones. That was quite an order as the older boys and girls fooled around with each other and the young ones had to fend for themselves. Two steps out past your waist and you could be over your head. I was bobbing for the third time when Bev noticed me and pulled me in. Those two boys were our heroes. Bev taught me how to snare rabbits, which we sold for tobacco money. Gerald taught me how to fish the brook back by the railroad track. He shared his best fishing spots as we ran in and out between the alders to find a little pool at the end of the rapids.

Of course we always picked opposite mentors. "Come on Bev, you can beat him," I encouraged. "No he can't, no way, he is bending his knees," David replied. ten, eleven we all counted;

only two more, I encouraged, but my hero dropped to the floor. "Anyone got a cigarette?" Not a cigarette in the crowd, but someone had a book of papers and some matches. Dried maple leaves finely crushed up made a half descent smoke. I slipped Bev a few butts I found in my father's car ash tray. He could break them open and make a real cigarette out of them. Of course he would offer me a few puffs.

We all felt pretty important as we sat on the continuous plank seat around the back of the station, smoking and coughing and spitting as we listened to the senior boys tell what went on here last night. Of course we had all taken an oath not to tell anything we hear. Boys and girls together; smoking and drinking beer. Home made beer that someone in the neighbourhood had made and someone else stole a few bottles. Who did what to who was mostly fantasy but made for great sport. We could hardly wait to get a little older.

"Here comes the train," someone would shout. We would all run out to the platform to watch the big locomotive. It always had that big light on in the center, smoke was puffing out the stack and there was a small jet of steam coming out around the wheels on both sides. The engineer, sitting up high in the locomotive, would have his head out the window. The noise of the train was deafening and we vibrated up and down as we waved to the engineer. He would return the wave and give a few toots of the horn.

We all envied his job, such power, such responsibility. He went to Fredericton every day, shunting cars off at different sidings, for lumber products mostly. Sometimes he would drop off a few cars for pulpwood. Bryenton's store often had a car load of bag feed shunted in. The train would go by the switch and the brakeman would hop out of the caboose and unlock the padlock to turn the switch. He would give a hand signal to the engineer and the shunting would begin.

"When the freight train goes down, it is time to get home for supper." That was the rule. It was pretty hard not to notice and you had better have a good excuse if you didn't obey. There were no two sittings for supper and everyone had the same menu. Most of the food was produced on the little farms in our community. There was always a big pitcher of milk and home made bread. Home made butter; pickles and jams adorned the table. The potatoes and meat were off the farm also. Salmon was always a favorite and this fish came from our own river. We got most of ours from Willie Hubbard next door. A few of the other staples like flour and molasses, cheese and bologna came from Bryenton General Store.

There were eight of us at the table when all the family was home. Hubbard's next door had seven and every family ranged from four to ten children. The older siblings were responsible to look out for the younger ones. One didn't have to go too far to find enough kids for a ball or hockey game. There was no television or computers to take up ones time. However, everyone was taught responsibility and respect. We all had chores to do, the older girls helped with the house work like cooking and washing clothes. The boys looked after filling the wood box and milking the cows. Someone had to feed the chickens and gather the eggs.

The little community of Bryenton consisted of a couple dozen little farms. A one room school and a church were pretty well centered in the village. The farms were long and narrow; they ran north from the river approximately two miles. Most of the houses were a fair distance from the highway. Everyone had a barn and a woodshed. It was a pretty lonely road to walk at night. One would notice a lamp burning in the window every now and then. Only the odd car would pass by maybe every half hour. One had to only step out on the highway and be very quiet if you wanted to know where the rest of your friends were. There would be some laughing and whooping going on and the dogs would be barking. Listen a little closer and you could identify the voices and decide whether to join them or not.

The highway and the railroad ran through everyone's farm. There was a nice little trout stream on the back side of the railroad. Everyone kept a few cows and a horse. All the properties were cleared about half way back from the river. They needed pasture land and hay land, and a garden. There were lots of fences to keep up, besides the side lines there were both sides of the highway and railroad. Seems like someone's cows were breaking out all the time, of course the first place they would hit for was a neighbour's garden.

I don't think anyone was particularly fond of cows but they were essential for their milk and butter. If one had to keep cows they might as well keep a few extra for their cream. During the summer months there was a surplus of milk. This was a good thing, the milk was separated and cream was put in the cream can. It had to be kept in a cold place like a spring or ice house. When the can was full it was taken to the station platform to go on the express early in the morning. The express ran a couple of hours earlier than the freight. It picked up passengers and cream cans and exchanged mail bags. Uncle Everett always met the train to pick up the mail as his family ran the store and post office. He always helped the conductor on with the cans. At the end of the month every shipper received a little cheque from the Capital Co-op in Fredericton.

Cows required a lot of care; they needed to be milked twice a day. In winter they were kept tied up and their stalls had to be cleaned out and fresh bedding placed. Of course they had to have fresh water and hay twice a day also. In summer they moved the pasture and someone had to go to fetch them for the milking. There were only one or two bulls in the neighbourhood. It was quite common to see an older boy leading a cow down the road with a bunch of young lads following. They would all have to witness the bull fix up the cow. There would be a lot of comments and cheering as the bull did his job. If no one was in a hurry they would stay for another round to the amusement of the spectators.

I'll always have fond memories of growing up in Bryenton. There were always lots of kids to play with. We played on the river paddling boats and skipping lightly across the logs that were in the boom. Sometimes we would hitch a ride on Jack Bell's tugboat as he pulled boom logs up to the men rafting the large rafts for the various lumber companies who had sawmills down river.

There used to be a lot of activity on the river in front of

Bryenton. All logs used to be cut in the winter. Then in the spring, after the ice had run, the logs would be dumped into the river. They would float down to the boom to be sorted and rafted. The boom started at the upper end of Bryenton and it was attached to boom blocks. These blocks were built with timbers and rock and could withstand the spring ice flows. The blocks divided the river, the South side would be jammed full of logs while the North side had a number of set nets reaching far into the river.

There was a Boom House on the South side, the Chelmsford side; it was just across from the Derby Station. Here the logs were sorted and made into rafts to be towed on down by tugboat. This made summer employment for men from both communities. It was common to see up to fifty men working on the logs. They wore heavy leather boots with sharp calks so they would grip on the wet logs. Most would take off their shirt and work with the top half of their underwear showing. From a distance it looked like they wore white shirts. They worked hard all day in the heat; then they often walked three miles to their home.

After a hard week of work it was time to blow off some steam. They would get all slicked up and take their woman to town. Of course they had to walk to the station to await the little three car train called the Dungarvon Whooper. It made a special run on Saturdays picking up passengers at every little station. The stations were about three miles apart. Most people would gather a little early to socialize with their neighbours, get filled in on community news. Some men might share a drink from a pint they kept under their jacket. "Prime the pump," they would say with a wink, as they offered the drink. Everyone was in a happy mood by the time they boarded the Whooper, on their way to see a movie or take in a dance at the Legion. I often wonder what shape they were in when they returned late at night. Anyway, they had

Sunday to sober up and they would all be back to work on
Monday.

These same men worked in the lumber camps during the
winter. They only got home to see their families on the weekends
and in many cases only once monthly. They still made the most
out of Saturday nights by going to town on the Whooper.
Somehow they managed to set a little aside to get married and
build a little place of their own. Quite often they would be given
one acre off the farm. It always fronted on the highway as no one
liked the long walk through the snow in the wintertime.

Eventually the highways were upgraded and logs began to
be trucked from the woods to the sawmills. A bus line was created
from Blackville to Newcastle. It ran daily and picked up
passengers right at their gate. There was no more walking to and
from stations. More people began driving automobiles. A new
pulp mill was built in Newcastle and men from all communities
gained steady employment at top wages.

More people became able to build homes so more building
lots came off the family farm. Eventually everyone left the farms
for an easier living. The Northumberland Co-op started a milk
delivery throughout the country, no one needed cows anymore.
The pastures grew up in alders and reverted back to forest.

Are we better off? I think not. We lost the log booming
industry. The railroad took off the passenger train; then a few
years later the freight trains stopped running. Finally the rails
were removed and parts of the railroad are now a walking trail.
The salmon nets have been removed from the river, gone are the
days when Mr. Hubbard used to net a half dozen shimmering
salmon. We used to help him place them in the ice house and
cover them over with damp sawdust.

Houses are more comfortable now, much larger with oil
heating. The garage replaces the woodshed. Every house has one
or two cars. The kids are bussed to schools. Stress is more

common as people buy on credit and then worry about the payments. I think everyone is working for the oil companies. It would sure be nice to see children playing together again. And it would be nice to see people associating and laughing together with their neighbours like they once did.

Paul McAllister

CHRISTMAS SPIRIT

Anytime after Halloween the merchants start to decorate for Christmas. The public is quick to follow. It is accepted that one should start seriously shopping now. You have had three hundred and sixty-five days and now there are only about fifty shopping days left. Where has all the time gone, first thing it will be Christmas and we have to buy for everyone. Panic starts to set in, where shall we start; and who wants what this year.

Strangely enough money never seems to be a problem. The gifts have to be bought anyway; the money will come from someplace. It always has and always will, I guess. Mary is the finance manager in our family. If it were me there would be some pretty meager gifts. That is why I don't shop or try to tell her how to either.

I am generally given the choice every weekend to go to the mall with her or stay at home by myself. I work all week and there are plenty of things I can do around home. However, she will remind me that she is only going to pick up a few things and we could be home early. Since it is generally mid-morning before we get started I start thinking of dinner. It would either be a nice meal at a restaurant in town with fries and gravy or I could stay at home and make myself a bowl of soup or a hot dog. I know how the day will go, I have been tricked so many times, but I fall for it again and go along for the drive.

The first hour is not bad. We walk down the corridor of the mall together. Oh, she will stop and step into the odd store to look at something for a few minutes. I wait at the entrance and watch the shoppers pass by. We exchange hellos with people we know. Mary generally picks up a few things at the drug store along with the Telegraph for me. I like to read the stories in the Reader section. Sometimes the Curtis boys have a short story. I may get a chance to read it while I wait for her. She usually buys a few small things before lunch. Sometimes we eat in the mall, but it is nice to get out of there so we go to a nearby restaurant.

After lunch I am anxious to get home, I have things to do and it is a nice day. But no, she has to do more shopping, besides there are some things she really needs for the house. So it is back to the mall. I might as well let her go as stand behind her; I am of no help to her anyway. My advice, generally based on the price, is not appreciated at all. Mary can go into a department store and disappear for a good hour or so. I try to find an empty bench to sit down; by this time my legs are killing me. I don't know what it is but I can walk for hours anywhere else, but only a short time in a mall.

Sometimes a man will take the other end of the bench to wait for his wife. In most cases we can start a conversation over the weather or the large crowd of shoppers out already. By the time one of our wives show up to claim us we are good friends. We know all about each other, where each live and what the economy is like in our communities. We generally have time to take a kick at the government or insurance companies ripping us off. In fact we are just getting into a good conversation when we have to say good day.

Just because they emerge with a few packages doesn't mean they are ready to go home. No way, just up the corridor it is the same thing all over again. Why does it take so long to make a decision? I can go into a store and pick up a couple of pairs of socks and a pair of work gloves and be out in five minutes. Women have a sixth sense when it comes to shopping. They know what each grand-child likes, needs, and even their favorite colour. I guess that is why they get so pre-occupied when they start shopping.

Mary starts shopping for the most distant relatives first.

You gotta make sure they get their presents on time. Just the other day Mary found the perfect toy for our latest grand-child, one year old Cameron. It was listed at sixty-five dollars at one store. Another store was running a special on them for fifty-four, I happened to be with her on this one. Judging by the size of the box I would think it would cost about twenty dollars to mail it to Grande Prairie. "Why don't you send him a card with a gift certificate for Zellers? They have a much bigger store than here," I suggested. She wouldn't hear of it.

"How would you like a gift certificate for Christmas?" she asks.

For a moment I thought it would be wonderful. I could get by with three less sweaters per year, to say nothing of the oversized off-colour shirts I receive, but I said the right thing. "I guess it wouldn't be very nice, no presents to open up, that wouldn't be much fun."

"My point exactly," she beamed.

A couple of evenings later she had bought enough coloured paper to cover the box. She sat it in the middle of the table and called me out from watching T.V.

"I need your help out here," she commanded. "Here, hold your thumb on here while I put some tape on." She taped it up well and placed some Santa Claus stickers on the parcel. Next she went over it with plain brown paper. Then she addressed it to Mr. Cameron. "How old do you have to be to be a mister?" I asked.

"Don't ask such foolish questions; there now we can mail it tomorrow."

Next day I tote the large box into the post office. There were eight people ahead of me doing the same thing. Everyone was trying to get ahead of the threatened Christmas postal strike. Mail early just to make sure was the idea. Most everyone was putting a one hundred dollar insurance on their parcel. We were no exception, and it cost us twenty-nine dollars and thirty cents to mail.

"There now, that is over with," she sighed, as we returned to the car. "I should have wrapped his birthday gift and mailed it at the same time," she commented. "After all, his birthday is Dec. 29Th, you know. Did you see the sweet little jacket I bought him?"

"Why didn't you stuff it in the same box?" I asked.

Now that was a stupid question.

FORERUNNERS

My neighbour is an elderly lady. Our two houses are set back off the highway twice as far as the rest. We share the same driveway and keep an eye on each other. "Would you mind taking a look over my way before you go to bed," she asked. "Just to see if everything is alright." Then she added that, "you know the other weekend that you and Mary went away. Well that night about three o'clock in the morning I heard three loud knocks, it sure startled me, I never got up."

"There must be some logical reason," I tried to comfort her. "You know these old houses sometimes creak and crack in the cold weather, I know mine does sometimes."

"No it was three loud knocks," she insisted. "You know I have been living alone here for the last twelve years. I was never nervous as long as I could see a light on over at your place. Now who would be out prowling at that hour of night? For sure they wouldn't want anything I have," she joked.

"Forerunner" came to mind, but I didn't dare mention the word. "Just give me a call if anything disturbs you," I offered in comfort. It was only a few days after that I heard her repeat the same story to Mary when she learned we were going away for another weekend to our daughter's place.

Now I feel kind of guilty about leaving her alone. If she wasn't so independent she could call a grandchild to stay with her if she's nervous.

"Yes, but its only when we go away," Mary reminded me.

"I don't think you should tell her when we are going. We could put a timer on a lamp and she will think we are home," I suggested. "She keeps insisting it was a knock," I laughed, "I had a notion to tell her it must have been a forerunner."

"A forerunner," Mary questioned, "what's that?"

"You mean you don't know what a forerunner is. It's like an omen, or a prophesy that something is going to happen. Why it's just a superstition, I think, but the old people used to believe in them, especially the Irish. The men in the lumber camps believed, if a horse got himself free and ran out to the hovel by himself; that was a sign that someone from that camp would have a fatal accident before spring. They were usually associated with death; a good storyteller knew lots of forerunners."

"I might have been considered a forerunner myself back about twenty years ago when I used to drive a road grader."

"Oh, come on now," she scoffed at me.

"You remember it always seemed to snow on the weekends. How I would hate to leave home at ten o'clock at night to go out into the storm to start plowing. I always expected someone would take a shot at me for up-ending their mailbox. My boss warned me not to turn out for mailboxes. "That bunch back Hill Top road all have their mailbox on truck rims and they generally take them in when a storm is on. After the plow goes by they set it up on the side of the road again. In that way they don't have to keep a mailbox shoveled out, not like a fixed mailbox. Sometimes they get careless and leave it out, if you cut around it they just sit it out further on the road, first thing the mailbox will be half way out on the highway," he cautioned.

"At first it didn't bother me much to up-end the odd mailbox. As the winter grew on I realized that this was the third or fourth time I up-ended their mailbox. When I was winging back the bank as I plowed the old mailbox would take a half a dozen tumbles ending up on top of the bank down the road a distance. The old grader took some time to get up to top speed of fifteen miles per hour. Sometimes I would just get a good speed up and I would meet a car where there was a mailbox. It was just a case of the box in the right place, but at the wrong time.

It finally began to play on me that some loon might be waiting to get even. It was not like I was whizzing by in a truck. There was lots of time as they could see my revolving light coming a half mile away. I could be a sitting duck sitting up on my bar stool sort of a seat in the middle of my glassed in cage in the centre of the grader. I think that is the real reason I didn't do any more plowing after that year.

It was a lonely job anyway; I never had anyone to talk to. "Just make sure the road is plowed so people can get to work in the morning," my boss ordered. He wasn't much concerned that the brakes were poor on the machine. "What do you need brakes for?" he questioned, "Just drop the blade if you need to stop." "How about a little more heat," I begged, "you can see your breath all the time." He promised he would see what he could do. "Anyway you have that little fan to keep the windshield clear, it works, doesn't it?" "Yes, it keeps a little spot open," I agreed.

Frost bumps were a real pain, if I had a good speed when the rear wheels raised up on the bump the blade under the middle would raise up. When the back wheels came down they would rise up again on the snow that emptied out of the blade when it rose. This caused a ripple effect as the grader bounced along the road. Of course the traffic would get the same effect. There was only one cure for the rabbit hops. Slow right down and start shifting up again.

I had about fifty miles of highway to keep clear. The last three miles down river from Irish Settlement was all woods with one house beside the river at the end of the road. It was an old rundown house that housed a large welfare family. The owner lived in town and was collecting rent for this old house at the government's expense. Not only did I have to keep them plowed out but they had all the services. The school bus and the mailman served them too. The family renting liked the privacy. I suspect he was in the agriculture business growing a little weed. Anyway it was generally night time when I turned in his yard. I had to look out for his two old derelicts of cars as his two dogs charged my machine, barking up a storm.

One night when I started plowing it was quite mild, the snow was packy. It was beginning to turn to rain as I passed through Irish Settlement about midnight. I had just turned the machine and started back when I discovered a rear tire went flat. There were no cell phones then so I had to walk for help. I didn't want to go back to that welfare house with the two dogs in the night; I didn't even have a flashlight. That was nobody's fault but my own, I carried one after that.

Anyway, I started walking up the road in the cold rain. I got quite heated up with all my heavy clothes on. My clothes became heavier and heavier as I started to get wet through. It was about two o'clock when I reached the settlement; everyone had gone to bed hours ago. I was thinking I would have to go to one of the houses and ask to use their phone, but I didn't know anyone. I may have upset their mailbox and that also entered my mind.

Just then I caught the glimmer of a light up at the other end of the village. I kept my eye fixed on the house as I trudged along. The old abandoned schoolhouse and an unkept graveyard were centered in the community. As I passed by I could imagine all the names on the stones as Kelly, Hogan, Clancy or Barry. These names were the only families left in existence here.

As I approached the house I noticed light in all the windows downstairs. Must be a party going on, they will likely invite me to stay until my ride picks me up. Perhaps they will offer a nice strong drink to take the chill off, I could sure use one right now. I never paid much attention to the fact that there was only one car in the driveway. I walked right up to the front door and gave a good loud rap so I could be heard above the party noise.

There was no response, I listened and there was no noise within. What kind of a party is this, I questioned, are they all scared to open the door, do they turn off the music and sit quiet hoping I will go away. A strange place indeed, I was thinking, as I stood there starting to look around. My questions were soon answered as I glanced to the left of the door. There was a fresh wreath of flowers attached to the house.

I was interrupting a wake; there would be someone inside sitting up with the remains according to tradition. Because there was no traffic on the road, and no car turned into the driveway, they knew it was nobody. The rap sent chills up their spines as they pictured the grim reaper at their door. I stood there for a little while in case someone might answer, then I would apologize and ask to use their phone. Since no one came and there was still no noise inside I slipped out onto the highway again. I trudged along for another hour or so until finally a car came along. The driver had compassion and picked me up.

The man was curious why I was walking at this time in the morning. I told him my trouble with the flat tire; that I was walking half the night and I sure appreciated him picking me up. I didn't tell him about my going into the wake house. He told me he worked kind of an irregular shift at the hospital; that he was a boiler operator and he started at four o'clock in the morning. After a while I mentioned that there was a wake house back in the community. He said it was a Mrs. Barry, everyone expected Mr. Barry would go first but she beat him to it. He didn't expect the old lad would be far behind as they were a very close couple.

I thanked him for the ride as he let me out at the all night Irving station. Then I called my wife to come and pick me up as I needed to get some dry clothes on soon or I would catch pneumonia. I would get a tire company to go back and change the tire in the morning.

The widow Clancy or "Pat" as everyone called her was the community story teller. She had two beautiful daughters, and so the young men liked to gather at her place to listen to her ghost stories. She would start out by reminding them that there are two new graves in the cemetery this year. Then she would wonder out loud who the third would be. "People die in three's," she would sigh. First there was Mrs. Barry; then there was Mr. Barry only forty days later.

Of course I knew Mr. Barry would be next, when he told us about the four loud knocks on the door in the middle of the night when he was waking his wife. He said there was no one there; it was a forerunner coming after him. Four knocks, forty days, get it, one for each ten days. Boys you want to watch out for that grim reaper, she would cackle. She had a good time that year striking fear into the brave young lads. They would all leave the house together as no one wanted to pass the graveyard in case a forerunner would be waiting for them.

GOLD

"Gold! You know where there is gold?"

"Yes I do," says Tom.

Funny, the women were talking to each other without paying any notice to their men, until the word "Gold" brings them to a dead silence.

"Well maybe not the exact spot, but I know the general area."

"Just listen to him," says Mary, "two beers and he is hallucinating. The only gold he knows is on his finger, and sometimes I have second thoughts about that."

"All right, make fun if you want, but the laugh will be on you when Bob and I find the "mother lode".

Tom throws in that mother lode term, just to impress his audience of his mining knowledge.

"Bob and I," says Bob, "you mean you are going to share with me?"

"Well yes," says Tom, "40-60 if you help me find it. Besides, there will be too much for just one person."

Bob always thought about a job change, but mining for gold just wasn't what he had in mind. Professional golfer was more to his liking.

"What makes you think you can find it?" Bob asks. "And where do we go to get it?"

The women are the quietest they have been all night, they are practically sitting on the edge of their chairs.

"Man-eater Mountain."

"Man-eater Mountain; where's that?"

"That is what we have to find out, but I have a general idea."

"Tell us more," says Liz. Bob's wife's eyes were sparkling with excitement. Bob was starting to lose enthusiasm; he had mental pictures of wheelbarrows, pick-axes, sweat and flies.

"Ah," says Mary, "Tom's dreaming out loud again."

"Pass me another beer there Bob, and I'll tell you the story."

They all pull up to the table and the storyteller begins.

"My father told me this story shortly before he died, he had always intended to do some prospecting but time ran out on him. He said the story was told to him by an older gentleman, a man he knew and trusted well. This man told Father the story but said no one talked about it much. You might call it superstition, but they thought gold was bad luck.

It seems a group of six men were going up to the head-waters of the Little South West River. They figured it to be a two day walk from their lumber camp to where they wanted to go. Their boss thought he knew a short cut but became lost. They travelled for two days and used up their provisions. That night they made shelter on the side of a mountain. They made a lean-to to sleep in and made a lovely big box fire. They were very hungry and they were grumbling at their leader for getting them lost. One of the men jokingly said, if we don't find the river, and the bear house, they would have to eat their boss, who was a skinny little man.

One of the crew was gifted, he was a natural artist. He took
a blackened wood coal and drew a picture of a big man stuffing this little man into a big boiling pot. He drew this on the side of a big white birch, and the old man said you could easily identify the two characters.

You see, this is how it got its name, Man-eater Mountain, says Tom".

"Yes, but what about the gold," says Mary.

"Did they eat the man?" asks Liz.

"One minute," says Tom, taking a long haul of beer, enjoying all the individual attention.

"No, they didn't eat the man. The next morning they came to the river and found the bear house intact".

"But the gold," Mary interjects.

"Oh yes, the gold. Well you know the bonfire they built on the side of the mountain."

"Yes."

"Well, they were wet and cold so they made a big bonfire out of porcupine beech."

"Porcupine Beech?"

"Yes, porcupine beech is probably the hottest fuel wood you can find. Those old camp cooks would kill for it. Well, they found a beech the porcupine had killed and it was as dry as flint so they used it on the fire. A breeze came up and it fanned the fire onto the rock on the back side of the fire. Some liquid or lava began to weep out of the rock, when it cooled off later that evening there were half a dozen golden nuggets hardened onto the rock.

Of course they thought it was gold, and they planned on sharing the loot the next morning, after they had a chance to cool off. So they went to sleep, but when they woke up the nuggets were gone. At first they thought they must have detached from the rock when they cooled off. In spite of all their sifting through the ashes not one nugget could be found."

"Where did they go?" asks Liz.

"They were on the rock when John Matthews added some wood to the fire in the middle of the night, so he said. But it was the general feeling that John took them all for himself when the rest were sleeping. This John was a shady character and they wouldn't put it past him."

"What did John do with them, Tom?" asks Bob.

"He didn't."

"What do you mean he didn't?"

"The poor devil drowned before the drive reached the settlement."

"Did anyone ever go up to that place again?" asks Liz.

"Not to my knowledge. Father's friend said the crew were pretty well broken up about what happened to John. He told Father he planned to go himself, but wasn't sure he could find the place again, and to tell the truth he kind of figured John's ghost might be up there watching over the gold."

"Wow, some story!" says Bob, setting another round on the table. "Where do you suppose Man-eater Mountain is?"

"Well," says Tom. "We know it is somewhere up at the headwaters, of the Little South west. And it is about a half day's walk from the river. A man, say, would walk about two miles per hour over rough territory; I would say 8 or 10 miles from the river."

"And it is on the side of the mountain," says Mary.

"The whole mountain may be full of it," says Tom.

"Christmas Mountains," says Bob.

"You guessed it," says Tom, "but which one - Donner or Blitzen?"

"Or Dancer or Prancer," says Liz.

"We can probably drive right to it with a half ton now, with all the lumbering going on up there.

But how are we going to find which one, that big old birch with the picture will be long gone now," says Tom. "I figure this incident must have happened about the early nineteen hundreds."

"Tiger Torch," says Tom.

"Tiger Torch, what's that?" asks Liz.

"That is a very hot flame throwing propane torch. I figure we go up there with a couple of bottles of propane and a tiger torch, heat up a few rocks and pick up the nuggets."

Everyone had a great laugh, and the women start to put a lunch on the table.

Bob and Tom talk about the legalities; income tax, staking claims, starting a mine and selling shares. But first they had to find the gold.

"Open up that bottle of Lobster, Liz," says Bob, "I think we can afford to splurge a little tonight. Oh! Oh! What if the mountain is already staked, - did you open that bottle already?"

At lunch they talk some more and what should they call their mine. Let's see, if we could put all our initials together it might make a name if we arrange them the right way. Finally they all agree on one name - Rainbow Gold Mining Co. We will all be millionaires soon.

"Did you tell anyone else about this?" asks Mary. "How come I never heard this story before?"

"Only one, it is something I was keeping in my back pocket."

"Who did you tell?" asks Bob.

"Johnny," says Tom.

There was complete silence for a moment. "But," Tom added, "He had been sick for quite a while."

"Time to go,' says Mary.

"Best Saturday night we've had in a long time, we will have to get together soon and make plans," says Bob.

"Well, think it over and let me know in the morning if you are in or not," says Tom, bidding them good night.

"I'll call you in the morning, Tom, good night."

Next morning Bob calls as promised.

"What day is it?" says Tom.

"Sunday," says Bob, "You didn't drink that much last night, how do you feel?"

"Good... good... but what date?"

"Why, it is the first of April, '95.""Hello - you still there?" What's he laughing about. "You son of a bitch!"

"I'm sorry," says Tom, trying to apologize.

"Not as sorry as you are going to be," says Bob. "I just wrote a letter of resignation and Liz has been looking in the catalogue for the last hour. Good day!"

Mary overheard the conversation and lit in on Tom.

"And you say you don't have any friends, well you have two less now, - no, make that three. You can get your own breakfast and dinner too, for that matter."

Sometimes you just can't win, thought Tom, the best April fool joke I ever pulled. But I guess the joke is on me.

ANOTHER GOLD STORY

A month later, Tom and Mary are visiting Bob and Liz again. Tom had to phone back and explain that the gold story really was true. He had thought that it was a good idea to April fool his friends, seeing that the day following the story fell on April fool's day. That is why he pulled the joke, at any rate; he had lost some of his credibility. By this time everyone had pretty well forgiven him, and they were all in good spirits.

They were having a business meeting. The first business meeting of the executive of the Rainbow Gold Mining Co. Tom appointed himself as President, Bob could be V.P., Liz said she would be secretary and produced a new scribbler to take notes. "Mary, you can be treasurer," says Tom.

"Yes, sure," she says "you are looking for someone to sponsor your prospecting venture."

"We will all share in the expenses," says Tom.

"Does that mean 40/60 for me, since I only have 40%?" asks Bob.

"Just a minute, Mr. Chairman," says Mary. "If you have 60% and Bob has 40%, where do Liz and I fit in? Seems like, we are just taken for granted, as usual."

"Never thought, I would need an auditor and a lawyer for our first meeting. Don't worry; you will get your fair share. Maybe it would be easier if we were equal partners. What difference would it make as long as we find the gold?"

"Now we can get down to business," says the Chairman, thumping his beer bottle on the table. "The snow will be all gone up there in a couple of weeks, and we should be ready to go. Let's list the provisions we will need, - make a list there, Secretary. Remember we should be able to claim all our expenses against our income tax."

"OK."

"Maps, lots of maps," says Bob.

"Propane," says Mary.

"Elephant torch," says Liz.

"You are in the right church Liz, but the wrong pew."

"Tiger torch is what we need." - They all have a good laugh.

"OK, should we get two?"

"Not yet, don't want to arouse too much suspicion," says Tom.

"Where are we going to stay?" asks Mary.

"I suppose we should have a tent."

"You mean we will have to buy a tent?" she asks.

"I can get a good discount if I buy it through work," says Bob, "as long as I pay cash."

"Where will we sleep, on the ground?" asks Liz.

"We will need some inflatable mattresses and sleeping bags too."

"I would rather use blankets," says Tom with a wink to Bob.

"I saw that," says Mary, -"one track mind!"

"How are we going to finance this venture?" Mary asks. "If we each put $500 in the pot, that should get us started. If we hit pay dirt we will buy a travel trailer. We still need a few more things."

"Like what?"

"Oh, a few buckets, picks and shovels and a fire extinguisher, don't want to start any forest fires."

"And we need a few groceries, if we are going to stay two nights," says Liz.

"You girls can look after that," says Bob.

The women start on their grocery order and what they will need from home. The men decide they could leave home right after work Friday night so they can set up camp and get a look at the country. They agree to be ready to go in two weeks time.

The days go quickly by, and right after work Bob and Liz arrive with their half ton loaded. "We have everything but the kitchen sink, Liz even wanted to bring that old chesterfield from the shed," Bob says with a laugh.

"Mary has enough stuff here for a week," says Tom.

"Bob and I will go ahead and you and Liz can follow in your truck. Just one more stop, - to get some ice and beer."

"Thought you were going up to work," quips Mary.

"OK, all set, now remember don't let on where you are going, just let on we are going on a fishing trip."

"Good idea," says Bob, "but we haven't even got a fishing rod and license."

"I have a couple of rods and we can get our license when we stop for beer."

In a couple of hours they are pretty close to where they want to be according to their navigator, Bob, who has been studying the maps all the way up.

"This would be a good place to set up our tent," says Tom, pulling into a gravel pit beside a little stream.

"Good choice," says Bob, "the only level ground around. The girls can pan for gold in the creek, while we are out."

"What are you stopping here for?" the women ask. "Don't see any gold here, nothing but sand."

They agree to set up camp and they all get busy unloading the trucks. Next, they Bar-B-Q a few T-Bones, on their propane Bar-B-Q.   "First time I ever saw anyone cooking with a propane Bar-B-Q in the woods. But a good thing, I guess, less chance of starting a forest fire if everyone used them, anyway, it makes a good excuse for all the propane on hand."

They all take a little walk to admire the beautiful countryside. "So nice and peaceful up here," Tom tells them that Bob suggested that they should pan for gold while he and Bob are trying to find the right spot. At that they all roll their pant legs up and wade into the stream with tin pie plates. After a few minutes and no luck they return to camp, to get ready to turn in.

Mary tells a story about Emily, her sister in law. "Seems, she was out at Dawson Creek, in the Yukon. It is now a tourist attraction and they give guided tours. Part of the tour, conducted by "Klondike Bill", was to have everyone do a little panning in the creek. Well you know Emily; she had bought a pair of gold nugget ear rings at the gift shop. So she slipped them into her pan. After a short time they were ready to keep on with the tour. Some had discovered the odd flake about the size of a pin head but nothing significant. They were all encouraging Emily to hurry along, but she was panning in the muddy water desperately looking for the other ear ring. She said she couldn't leave yet as she only had one and held up the gold nugget. She darn near started another gold rush, -they all went back to their pans. Klondike Bill's eyes nearly fell out of their sockets and he came over to look in Emily's pan. They all had a great laugh when she found the other ear ring."

They try to settle in for the night, the women were complaining about the sleeping quarters, too quiet, too dark, mosquitoes, can't sleep.

"What's that noise?" asks Mary.

"Only an owl," Tom replied.

"What about bears?" asks Liz.

"Bears wouldn't touch you girls," says Bob, "you would complain too much."

One more hoot, just a little closer this time.

"I know where I'm going," says Mary, and she makes a bee line for the truck. "See you in the morning."

"Me too," says Liz as she takes the other truck.

"Whoever suggested bringing them up here?" asks Bob.

Next morning bright and early everyone was out walking around in the gravel pit, each kinked in a different direction, sore necks, sore backs and mosquito bites. Bacon and eggs for breakfast, the men are eager to heat up a few rocks on the hill up there.

"Now you girls stay here and we won't be too long," says Tom.

"You mean you are going to leave us here alone?" asks Mary.

"Why not, you are big girls," he replies, "Someone has to watch the camp."

"What if someone comes and wants to know what we are doing here?"

"Just tell them we are going fishing and will be back shortly," says Tom.

"Yes, fishing on the side of a mountain with a propane torch," says Liz.

"Well we don't want to give our secret away, what shall we say?"

"Say we are environmentalists looking for pre-historic fossils. Say we are looking for signs of tropical animals that roamed around the earth millions of years ago, before the ice age."

"Boy, that sounds like an excellent idea, Bob, we will call you professor Bob," says Tom. "Say you are doing research for U.N.B. and I am hired as your guide."

"OK," says Bob, "not much chance of anyone knowing me up here. Suppose they will buy the story?"

"Oh sure," says Tom, "I will just print U.N.B. on these shiny water buckets and propane tanks with this here marker, that should make it official."

"Best if they didn't see us at all though. If anyone is looking for us tell them we went the opposite direction. We will be back for first lunch at 10."

"Now how are we going to handle this, Bob? If I use the torch, you can go up on the hill with the field glasses and give me the signal if you see anyone on the road. That would give me time to put the torch in under the tarp on the back. If I hold the torch on a rock for 10 minutes it should heat it up enough to tell if there is anything. I don't expect we will hit anything right off, we will have to try different areas."

Tom tries his luck on a dozen different rocks, and decides this is not the right hill, so they pack up and return to base.

The women are sitting back in lawn chairs waiting for their men, who arrive, empty handed. They have coffee and the women say they are getting bored with nothing to do. Why can't they go out too, they might bring luck? They talk over their morning venture; this might take a long time finding the right hill.

This triggers a thought to Bob, and he suggests that they could go and pick up samples, bring them back to camp and they could take turns heating them up.

"Great idea," says Tom, "but how will we know which one came from where?"

"I will map and number the samples," says Bob.

Everyone agrees, -four heads are better than one.

Next trip out Tom and Bob leave the propane torch at camp and go out picking samples. One hour later they are back with all they could haul.

"OK, let's start," says Tom, lighting the torch. "I have enough here to last the rest of the day."

Bob sets them out in the sand in alphabetic order; then he takes out the map and shows the women how he marked them. "A is handiest right here at the bottom of the hill. H is up along the road 3.5Km on the speedometer, etc."

Tom starts at A with all standing around, no luck so he shifts to B, the help wanders off, and Tom is trying to think of an easier way. He figures he could set each piece up on this big old granite near by and position the torch to hit on the samples. They might heat up faster as the sand could be slowing down the heating process. This invention works good as after heating each piece, all he had to do was push it back over with a stick and place another on. He stays at it all afternoon but no luck.

They are all pretty discouraged come supper time, and there is even some talk that it was just a dream, "just not meant to be!"

Tom tries to keep their hopes up. It just takes time, that's what makes it so good when you find the mother lode.

"Mother lode, mother lode," retorts Mary, "I know where this mother is going. I am going home where I can get a good night's sleep in my own bed, there isn't any gold up here anyway, -only mosquitoes."

"That Mary is no outdoor girl," says Tom. "I guess we might as well break up camp, we can come back again next weekend Bob. Just you and I, if you like, we could gather some more samples and take them home."

They all agree and load up the trucks so they can get out before dark. They pick up all the garbage so they leave the site as they found it.

"What about that pile of burnt rocks?" says Tom, "suppose anyone will figure out what was going on? We can throw them out of the way before we leave."

He and Bob scatter the rocks over to the side of the pit.

"What's this," says Bob, pointing to a little nugget in the sand where the pile of rocks had been. They all rush over to see the spectacle.

"Not Emily's ear ring is it Tom?" he says.

"No, honest, -don't know how I missed it. I guess it must have boiled out the back side of the rock. I didn't look on the back side. I used a stick to push them back over when they were done."

"Now I know what we will be doing next weekend," says Tom, and they all departed in high spirits. Rainbow Gold now has one nugget to their account!

GOLD III

Tom and Bob already had a nugget, but they weren't sure where it came from. Another expedition proved to be fruitless, no more nuggets, and the two were feeling kind of defeated. They didn't even know if they were near the right area or what kind of rock they should be looking for.

"Perhaps we need some expert advice, like a geologist or someone who has worked in a gold mine. Anyway, we have the winter to work on it. I will see if I can dig up some books on geology," said Bob.

"I know a geologist," states Tom. "He lives in Douglasfield, his name is, Ben Baldwin; we belong to the N.B. Soil and Crop Association. I think he is retired now, but he has worked all over the world. He is a very controversial chap, an environmentalist, you know. He is the only one around who dares to speak out about the pulp mills polluting the river and he is also associated with that group of college students protecting the harvesting of the Christmas mountains, but he is a man we could trust."

"Why don't we take a few of these rock samples to him and see if he will help us," says Bob.

They pick up four different samples, a rose and glassy speckled one, a greenish grey piece, a rusty brown with all kinds of little yellow flakes sparkling on the freshly broken sides, and a multi-coloured piece. "I know this piece is no good but we will throw it in anyway," says Tom, holding up a piece of granite. It looked like three separate rocks formed into one. It was black on one side. A piece of brown oxide seemed to fuse it to some white granite and another brown seam welded some grey slate stone to it.

"No, not much gold in that one," says Bob, laughing.

The two call on Ben and are invited in, and they tell him of their adventures. Tom goes over the old yarn of Man-eater

Mountain, that started this expedition. Ben is amused by the story, but not too excited.

"It was a favourite pastime of men in the lumber camps to make up stories about gold fortunes, something like people raving on about winning the lotto these days," he explained. "I have heard so many of them that I don't get excited anymore. A good rock sample is what excites me, even after all these years of prospecting."

They take the rock samples out of the bag and place them on the table, and ask Ben if he thinks there is anything worthwhile here.

"This one is useless, no mineral in it, - granite. This one has a little iron in it, enough to cause it to rust on the outside, but of no value."

"But what about all that gold flex on the broken sides?" asked Bob?

"Pyrite, - fool's gold. As some call it; worthless. Now this one looks a little better," he says, pointing to the greenish-grey. "It looks like it could have a little copper content. If any would have any gold it is more apt to be this one," pointing to the multi-coloured granite. "It is a piece off a volcanic rock. Notice how these pieces are all fused together."

The two amateur prospectors looked at each other. They were more sure than ever they need some expert help.

"Show him our nugget," says Tom, although they both agreed not to tell anyone about it. He knew Bob was just as anxious as he to show it to a professional.

"Nugget?" inquires Ben, as Bob pulls out the little velvet bag with the draw string on the top that their wives had presented them with after their find.

Bob empties the little nugget on the table, and Ben begins to laugh.

"What? Fools gold?" asks Tom, with a big frown on his

face.

"No! Copper," says Ben.

"Gold is yellow, notice how orange this is."

"You know," says Bob, "I thought it was quite a bit darker than when we discovered it."

"Yes, it has turned darker," says Tom, "what a letdown."

"Not necessarily so," says Ben, "have you noticed the stock market price lately? Gold prices are away down, about $330, an ounce. Copper, on the other hand, is at an all time high."

"I am convinced more than ever we need help, if we are ever to get this thing off the ground," says Bob.

"Yes, would you be interested in going in with us?" says Tom. "We haven't any money to pay you with. Do you ever work on commission?"

"In fact, I am doing some work for a group up Bathurst way on commission right now, and I have a group over in Newfoundland working for me. I generally work on a 50-50 basis."

Tom looks at Bob and Bob gives him the O.K. nod. Half a loaf is better than none, they figure.

"You're in," says Tom, offering Ben his hand, and Bob does the same.

"When can we start?" asks Tom.

"We should go up and do a little prospecting next spring," says Ben. "About the end of May; before the leaves, are out on the hardwoods and hopefully before mosquito season. In the meantime I will look for anomaly maps of the upper Little South West area. I will do some research to see if there were ever any sightings of metal up there."

On their way home Bob and Tom review the events of the day. They are no longer owners of Rainbow Gold Mining Co. From now on they will only own fifty percent. But for a small company they have a full fledged geologist, not many prospectors can make such a boast.

"Let's not tell our wives about the nugget," Tom suggested. "They would probably lose heart. Whoever heard of a copper nugget anyway?"

Things were pretty quiet over the winter. Tom and Mary continued to socialize with their business partners, Bob and Liz. However, whenever the subject of gold would come up the men would be quick to caution them not to get their hopes too high.

Over the winter Tom had two encouraging events happen to him.

The first was when he confided in a good friend and woods forester for Miramichi Pulp and Paper that he was doing some prospecting in the Pole river area. He then asked if he had ever heard of Man-eater Mountain. The forester replied that he knew exactly where it is. "You can line up Quaguar and Mullin Stream lakes from the road at the top of Man-eater," he said. "In fact I can get you some large scale company maps with Man-eater and all the surrounding roads marked on it."

The other thing to confirm his faith in Ben happened while he and Mary were on a vacation out west. One day at the West Edmonton Mall Tom noticed a glassed in rock display in a centre court. He studied the rock samples while Mary was doing a little shopping. A dark green shiny one contained a high percentage of copper. Although there were a hundred or more samples labelled there the one that most resembled the multi-coloured sample they had shown Ben, was labelled to be found in gold mines.

The two prospectors kept close watch on the activities up Christmas Mountain way, as they would be working near the area. This would be the second year for the protesters, who are trying to stop the lumber companies from cutting the oldest stand of lumber in the Province. There are some species of animal and plant life in these mountains that are extinct in the rest of the Province. However, the pulp mill companies claim that they need this wood to keep their industry going, if this lumber is not cut soon it will only blow down, as it is old growth and is over mature.

The protesters were more vocal this year and seemed to be gaining more support from various environmental groups. As their scheduled date with Ben, to look at the mountain, grew near, they heard on the news that the Iroquois Warriors had joined the protesters and were disrupting the trucking from Christmas Mountain.

Finally the day arrived, Bob still had a few days left to teach, so Tom agreed to accompany Ben by himself. He waited at home for Ben, expecting they would both go up in his half-ton. Ben stopped in and suggested they could meet up there at the bridge that crosses the Little South West, as he was going on from there that night. He also had to stop, for a few minutes, at a camp on the way up to visit some people he knew.

Tom proceeded on his way up the Plaster Rock road, with the radio on; he learned that the encounter between the Iroquois and the company had intensified. He envisioned all kinds of trouble, perhaps he wouldn't be allowed up the Catamaran road. He would probably be considered an activist since he wasn't working for the Company. Who would believe him if he said he was prospecting. Can't say I am going fishing, he thought, no fishing gear. Well, one thing for sure, Ben is ahead and if they let him through, I shouldn't have any trouble.

On entering the Caterman road he noticed quite a few placards stuck up along the road. "Protect the Christmas Mountain." "Stop cutting on Christmas," and so on. Just my luck to be caught in the middle of this feud, he thought, as he donned a dark pair of sun glasses and pulled his big straw hat down as much as allowed good visibility. Wouldn't be surprised if they have video cameras set up to see who is using the road.

A few miles up the Catamaran Tom rounds a turn and comes

upon a blockade. The road wasn't completely blocked, but one had to drive cautiously to pass through, it would be almost impossible for a big pulp truck to get through. There were big piles of wood and rocks, projecting out about three quarters of the width of the road, first from one side and then the other. About half a dozen of these obstacles were being manned by the Iroquois. Tom noticed a dozen or more braves dressed in battle dress, green and khaki combat outfits with big hunting knives attached to their belts. They looked like soldiers except for their head bands and long black pony tails. Tom proceeded through with caution, and was relieved to see a few return his wave. He never expected to see them set up there, almost at the mouth of the road; he thought they were joined up with the college protesters up at Birch Lake, fifty miles on up the road at the Christmas Mountains.

Finally Tom reaches the bridge and Ben joins him in the truck, they look at the map and figure Man-eater is about five miles. Tom drives and Ben surveys the rock which lines the ditches all along the way.

"Granite," says Ben, "not a very likely place to find any mineral, granite everywhere."

Tom's hopes of finding a strike begin to fade, as he proceeds along the way.

"Humm," says Ben, "it's changing, notice how these rocks have some rust on them, - very interesting."

"Well, there she is," says Tom as they start to ascend the mountain "looks like a big gum drop, not rough like some of the other hills nearby."

"Yes, quite impressive," says Ben. "Stop the truck; I want to break some rock."

Ben gets out his old sledge hammer, and beats a fist sized piece off of a rusty grey flat mosser that is half projected out in a little stream. He holds it up with one hand and scrutinizes it looking through his magnifying glass.

"Anything?" asks Tom.

"Patience," says Ben, "you need lots of patience for this job. Some days you don't find any good samples at all, but sometimes you get lucky. I am going to walk a little; I'll meet you at the top of the mountain." He walks along the side of the road, every now and then stepping off to knock a sample off of an interesting rock. Every now and then he would put a sample into one of the canvas bags that he would label to be analyzed.

What a view from the top, you could see for miles all around. Just as Tom's friend had explained, there was Mullin Stream Lake and Quaguar right in line about ten miles off.

Tom walked down the logging road to meet up with Ben. He didn't know what to look for so he carried Ben's backpack of samples.

"What's this?" asks Ben, as he jumps across the ditch to examine another rock.

"Now where did this come from?" as he walks around the stove sized jaggedly blue rock. Geologist Ben Balwin examining an ore sample on Man-eater Mountain, early 1990's

"Notice this rock, Tom; it is different than all the rock around here.

It is a volcanic rock, the same kind of rock you find up around Brunswick Mines."

"How can you tell the difference?" asks Tom.

"It is twice as hard as other rock, and very sharp." He hammers a sample off and holds it up to the sun. "There is mineral in this one all right. Notice the silver streaks in this rock."

"You mean those tiny little specks right there?" says Tom, as he rotates the sample around.

The two travel around in circles to see if they can find more of the same. At the end of the day no more could be found. However, Ben was not discouraged. "Not often one is that lucky on the first day," he exclaimed.

"Well, where do you suppose that rock came from?" asks Tom.

"It could have erupted from a volcano or dropped off a glacier thousands of years ago, I like the shape of that mountain though. We should do a little drilling to see what is really there."

"How can we afford that?" asks Tom

"I think I can convince a mining company to do some exploration," he says.

"How does that work?" asks Tom.

"Mining companies do exploration work all the time," he explains, it is an income tax write off for them. If they work your claim they will generally pay you five hundred dollars a claim for the first year. You should always retain five percent of the claim and they own the rest. If they should be lucky and find some interesting deposits, they will do more drilling the next year, and at this point you start to make some money, they will then pay five thousand a share, and after that you start to collect royalties if it is worth mining."

"When I get home tomorrow I will send these samples to be analyzed, and I will contact some mining executives, that I know, to see if they are looking for some more interests. I won't be going home tonight, as I will be spending the night with some friends of mine up at Birch Lake."

Tom lets Ben out of his truck and returns down the Catamaran road. He wonders what he will encounter at the road block. However, when he comes to the Iroquois camp everything looks natural. The roadblock has been removed and the camp abandoned.

He learned afterward that a bus load of R.C.M.P. accompanied by a bulldozer arrived at the scene that day. They served an injunction on the Iroquois and bulldozed off the barricades without any altercation.

About a week later Ben called Tom to advise him of his progress. The samples have been sent away but it will take a month to get the results. However, he had an American firm on the hook, and that we should stake at least ten claims surrounding the area of the find.

Since Bob was still teaching, he suggested that Tom should hire someone to replace him and he would pay his wages. Tom found a man called Ron who said he had experience staking claims, and hired him. Before they could start they had to go to the Department of Lands and Mines in Bathurst and obtain a license for prospecting.

A beautiful young woman clerk was very helpful in looking after their needs. She took them to the basement and photocopied maps of the area for them. Then she enlarged them with another machine. She was able to look up all the names of the registered claims that were registered in that area. Tom was interested in the claims that had been staked about thirty years previous because he knew his father Earl had staked claims in that area for his boss O'Brien Lumber Co. He was pleased to find a block of claims registered under the name Trafalgar. Trafalgar was one of the O'Brien Enterprise companies. The two left with their prospectors' license, a bunch of aluminum tags to place on each corner of each claim, a case of line ribbon, and lots of maps. Ron kept lamenting that they couldn't bring the girl, as she was so knowledgeable about staking claims. I am sure many a prospector, if they ever strike it rich, would willingly share a bit of their fortune with her, even if she was only a civil servant.

The next day Tom and Ron went up to stake claims. According to the book on mining instructions, it said to start at the N.E. corner, scratch on the aluminum tag supplied the date and hour of entry. Proceed 400 metres South to post #2, then 400 metres West to #3, then 400 metres North to #4, then 400 metres East to join up to post #1, then mark on tag #1 the time of completion along with the Prospectors license #. Each claim contains 32 hectares.

Tom was reading over the instruction manual, "Boy, this sure looks complicated," he says.

"Piece of cake," says Ron.

"Sure glad you have experience, Ron," he says.

"Not too much," says Ron, "I helped David Estey for a few days up at Little River in sixty-five."

"Well, at any rate you know more than I," Tom says.

Ron takes a look at the map and puts his finger down on a spot, "We start here," he says.

"Well, O.K.," says Tom, "but is that the North East corner? That is where #3 tag is supposed to go, isn't it?"

"Right," says Ron.

"Well, how do you mark the starting time?" Tom asks.

"Wing it," says Ron, "just figure out how long it will take us to have come from #1 and count back."

"Well, all right," says Tom, "but we don't want to be finishing before we start," he was totally confused by this time.

"Just follow me," says Ron, with compass in hand, "you flag the trees as you follow."

"400 metres," says Tom, "you counting?"

"Yes, don't talk or I might lose track."

I will count too, thought Tom, as he tries to keep Ron in sight, 400 metres should be close to 500 steps in this rough terrain. However, when he reaches 250 he wasn't sure if it was 250 or 350. Oh well, he thought, I will just have to trust Ron.

When he caught up to Ron at the corner post, he noticed he was carrying a twig, with five kinks in it. "So that is how you keep track of your paces," says Tom.

"Yes, I put a kink in the twig every fifty paces," says Ron.

"But you only have five kinks. How come?"

"Well, I only count my left foot; you don't have to count so high that way."

"This post #4 lets see - time finished will be 4 p.m. Next will be post #1, we should be there for 10 a.m.," Ron says with a laugh.

"If we get this claim done by 4 p.m., I will be happy," says Tom, "I am not in very good shape for all this walking over windfalls and breaks."

Now Tom had heard about Ron, someone had said about him, "There is a right way, and there is Ron's way." It seems he always has an alternative way to do things. Perhaps that is why he wasn't working much lately. I just hope he doesn't get these claims all mixed up, as I would hate to have to go over them all again, he thought.

Two weeks later they had eleven claims finished, and they decided to call it off till they had some positive word from Ben. Tom was quite satisfied to see the job finish as he was all scratched up and both shins were skinned from crawling over blowdowns. Besides, it cost quite a bit to drive as it was close to 300 KM return every day.

Ben recorded the claims and anxiously awaited the results of the sample tests, as his client was also anxious to see some extremely good test results before he would commit himself.

Finally Ben called Tom and Bob to drop in as he had received the results of the samples he had tested. The next day the two prospectors call on their partner. Ben laid out the sample sheets on the table; they were printed on large sheets from some mineral laboratory in Ontario. There were a lot of minerals and percentages listed. "This is the best one," Ben points out, "this was from that volcanic rock we found, Tom."

"How good is it?" Tom asks. I don't understand the sheets."

"Good," says Ben, "there is some copper, zinc and gold. Good but not exceptional. The problem is there are all kinds of equally good testings up around Brunswick Mines and Heath Steel. In order to entice a mining company to start in a new area we will have to find a better sample. But I am sure we can find more if we go back up there and do a little poking around."

"How much gold was there in that sample?" asks Bob?

"About one to a million," replies the geologist.

"Well, we will just have to find a better sample," says Tom, "or pull a Bre-X."

They all have a good laugh at that, and start to make plans for the next adventure.

GRANDPARENTS

When I was a young lad I was taught to respect my elders. An elder was anyone as old as or older than my father. You didn't call them by their first names, only Mr. or Mrs. Surname. Another thing, you were required to tip your hat to an elderly lady. These elders were the pillars of the community. They were the wise ones, they had "been there, done that." They always had lots of time and were willing to share their knowledge.

The elders in our community were honest hard workers. They were proud of their large families, their church and their community. Young men and women were taught many life skills by their elders. Just as they had learned from their parents or some respected elder.

Often when a young man thought he had enough schooling he would drop out to learn a trade under the watchful eye of an elder tradesman. Sometimes they worked together for years as the apprentice learnt from his senior. The new tradesman never pretended to be smarter than his teacher. In fact he would be content to wait his turn to come only after his mentor passed on. Many of the great trades like carpentry, fishing, lumbering and blacksmithing were passed down from one generation to the other.

Of course most of my generation graduated from high school and some even from college. Now at our age we have just become officially retired. Some have retired with a nice pension and some with less. At any rate most of us have reached the age of grandparents. Most of my elders have passed on and now it is my turn. How come no one calls me "mister" or wants to learn from my experience?

I content myself by blaming the computer. I know nothing about operating these machines. It seems like I am the only illiterate person around but, you know, you can't teach an old dog new tricks. They tell me if you push the right buttons you can find out whatever you want to know about any subject.

So who needs elders anymore, no need to tip your hat to the ladies or call the old men Mister. Young people are so smart these days they don't want to waste their time with old people. Besides they are making out okay by themselves. The elders have their own places and most have cars. They watch the old re-runs on T.V. and play cards. They even get to socialize each week at their Senior Citizen Clubs.

Who is going to show these young women how to cook or knit? Can you imagine them trying to make a quilt without a senior lady to show them how? Can a computer show a young man how to harness a team of horses or how to set a net? How about using a chainsaw to fell a tree?

"Get a grip," most young women don't have time to cook and knit. They are all professionals and have real jobs and earn a salary. They can buy whatever they need at the grocery chain stores or the malls. Men don't use horses around the farm or in the woods anymore. Lumber is harvested with computerized processors. These machines are programmed to get the most out each tree. From there the logs are loaded with hydraulic loaders and trucked to the various mills. When you think about it, fishing a gill net is illegal now. I can remember when salmon fresh out of our river was part of our summer diet. I guess if one wants salmon now they can buy a farmed one at the supermarket. They are good too, but any old timer will tell you, they are not as good as poached June salmon.

Well, there must be something seniors are good for? Can you guess what it is?

"Grandparents!"

"Grammy and Pappy" our grandchildren call us and they think we are wonderful. Of course the feeling is mutual; we love to visit back and forth. Grammy always has little gifts for each as they exchange hugs and kisses. Later they will show and tell of all their little achievements since the last visit. She can make a game of tidying up their room as they eagerly work together. After they will gather round her for a story from the new book she brought them.

I on the other hand am the outdoors man. They can generally find a bicycle that needs some adjusting. They help me find the tools as they explain in detail how it has been working. When it is finished I get the reward of their happy smiles. They think their Pappy can fix anything. When it comes to a tree fort or back yard rink Pappy is a specialist. He will labour endlessly as he tries to meet their approval. Once again the only acknowledgment necessary is their happy thank you as they try it out.

In conclusion, I would like to say that it really doesn't matter if those computer smart teenagers call me Mister or not. What I like to hear are the happy shouts of "Pappy and Grammy" when we meet. I think about them as I follow my wife through the children's clothing aisles at the Mall. She holds up little outfits wondering which grandchild could use it. I can get the same results by buying a bag of candy which is kind of "off limits." Their parents keep telling us that we don't need to keep buying them things but we enjoy doing it. No doubt it will always be that way as long as they keep calling us Pappy and Grammy.

HOMEMADE

Here's to you – happy memories! I raise my glass to my friends as we share a glass of home made. I hope they approve of the vintage. I like to watch the expression on their face as they sip the first taste. Some smack their lips and nod or smile but the odd one makes a face and pass the glass over to someone who likes it. Of course those who do this are not true wine connoisseurs. They expected it to taste like champagne, sweet and bubbly.

Most often my guest will comment on the taste- "kind of a nutty, fruity taste, very good." Another sips and a nod, "yes, very good. Do you have any for sale; I wouldn't mind having a bottle to take home to my friend who enjoys a good bottle of red wine."

"Sorry," I say, "I only have a few bottles of this brand left. Perhaps next year I may sell some as I have quite a stock of two year wine. You see, a good wine takes about three years to mellow up. I remember bottling some a few years ago that I gave serious consideration whether to throw it out. It was kind of sharp and sour, even bitter. I had a box of forty ounce bottles that didn't look very attractive so I filled them and settled them on the bottom rack. I figured I would likely pour them out eventually. So after three years I got up the courage to try one. You know what; it was one of my best grape wines. It had become mellow and full bodied with age."

People often ask me, what I make my wine out of. They have made some themselves out of a kit but it didn't have the flavour like mine. I compare making wine from a kit like painting a picture by numbers. It never gets real good but it never fails either.

When you make wine out of scratch you have lots of disappointments. Some batches would be too sweet. Some bottles would blow their corks. In fact the wine cellar was hardly a safe place to enter when the corks would blow and the contents foam out all over the place. Funny thing, the bottles would look alright for a month or two; then generally in a humid warm stretch of weather they would start to pop. The house would smell like a brewery. I would have to empty out the remainder of that batch and mop up the cellar.

I read books and recipes and try to make a better wine. However, you can't be sure of the results until you taste it. The more you read the more uncertain you are, because the recipes often contradict each other. Through trial and error I sometimes come up with a very pleasing bottle. I keep track of the contents and record the information on each bottle on a piece of masking tape at time of bottling. The information is generally in code as it is for my information only. 2 GIA 0 6 would indicate two parts grape and one third apple, makes a good wine. Equal parts of grape and apple make a light wine which I call Grapple. However, two parts apple and one part grape didn't turn out very good – too thin and bland.

Some of the best wine turns out by accident, such as my Raspberry-Rhubarb, which reads R + R 0 6 on my little bottle code. This happened by accident. My wife Sylvia decided to defrost the deep freeze. You know, much like house cleaning. There was a great number of plastic bags of raspberries, also rhubarb settled on the bottom; no man's land. "All the old stuff has to go," she declared, and chucked them in a five gallon bucket. I couldn't bear to see all that fruit go to waste. I remembered seeing recipes in a wine book for raspberries. There was another for rhubarb, one of the few vegetables they recommend. I blended the two together.

One of my favourite minister's likes a little sip now and then. I give him a couple bottles each Christmas. When we meet he remarks how well he enjoyed the wine and he has kept the bottles for me so I could fill them up again. I ask him which bottle he liked best. He replied he thought the one with two initials was better then the grape, both good though.

There is a lot of preparation to making wine from scratch. You have to be ready when the fruit is ripe. After picking it has to be crushed immediately. I use food grade white five gallon buckets to start the batch. After crushing I add a camdem tablet to sterilize the mash. This takes twenty-four hours. The sterilization kills the natural yeast which in most cases does not make good wine. After the first day I test the juice with a hydrometer. Next I add a sugar and water mixture to bring the scale up to the required reading for a twelve percent alcohol wine. It is a better keeper when the reading surpasses ten percent.

When this is done I then add brewers wine yeast. I set the buckets up next to the furnace to keep the contents at room temperature. Soon the batch begins to work, you can see the bubbles rising and breaking at the top. For the next few days it becomes more vigorous. I punch down the cud on the top a couple of times a day as the juice becomes thinner and bubblier. After about a week the sugar has completely turned to alcohol. I test with the hydrometer and when it reaches zero I strain the batch into five gallon glass carboys.

Since air is bad for wine I place air locks in these jugs. The locks allow the wine to continue working and the gas, which at first, is escaping fast at the rate of a bubble per second. In a couple of weeks the wine is settled, the bubbles stop and it is time to rack the wine. I keep my siphon a couple of inches from the bottom of the wine as I transfer the good wine to a clean five gallon jug. In a month's time the wine should be racked again. This time I can go a little closer to the bottom, maybe the siphon is only one inch from the bottom. Each time you rack you end up with less good stuff, which is why I like to start off with several buckets. I generally end up with a couple full fives and a couple of one gallon jugs as the containers must be kept full at all times.

I am always gathering wine bottles and my friends save bottles for me also. Cleaning is generally done in the fall outdoors. I soak them in twenty gallon Rubbermaid tubs for a day or two. There is a special cleaner for glass bottles, it is more like an acid than soap, very strong, wear rubber gloves or it will burn your skin. The directions call to rinse three times with clean water before using. I use the garden hose holding the bottle upside down. This makes the bottles sparkle like new. Then they are packed in clean garbage bags.

Some wet snowy day in the first of the winter, with the wood furnace heating the basement, I go to work bottling the vintage of the year. I generally get twenty-five bottles from a jug. Then I label them and put them to rest in the wine cellar for the next three years. They should be nice and mellow by then if I did everything right. I can only wait and enjoy the stuff that has aged.

I have a glass mostly every night and find some brands better than others. I refer to my records to note the cause for the different taste. I can only go by the taste that pleases me and that is what I try to achieve. Just today my barber handed me a few bottles she had saved for me. She said she and mother enjoyed the bottle and practically fought for the last glass. It was very good; we were trying to figure out what the R + R meant. They decided it must be rest and relaxation. She laughed when I told her it was rhubarb and raspberry.

Every time I have a glass I remember the fruit on the tree or vine just before the picking. Is there a more beautiful sight, I think not. I also remember the people I have shared my product with. Some have since passed but their memory of friendship and conversation still remain. Yes, there is a lot of work making wine from scratch but the reward is worth it.

HORSES

The first horsey ride I remember was on the toe of my father's boot. He would cross his legs and let me sit on his toe and he took me by the hands to balance me while he bounced me up and down. That was the best horse a three year old could have, father's attention and a horsey ride. My older brother would get a little more vigorous ride with a little bounce to represent a bucking horse. No matter how tired he was he never let up till we got a little horsey ride.

When we became school age we were able to go to the theatre to see a few Saturday afternoon matinees. Gene Autry, or Roy Rogers and Trigger would be on the screen. Sometimes there would be Cowboys and Indians doing battle. After that we would gallop around the outside of the house and woodshed shooting each other if we could get the drop on them. Father took notice to our antics and thought it would be fun if we had a real pony.

Next summer holidays we were surprised to see a truck drive in with a pony for us. Lady was a medium sized pony, black with a white star. She was thin and her coat was matted with a long unkempt mane and tail. She had just come in from the West, the horse dealer told father. She would make a nice pony if she received some care. She was sound, no vices like heaves or such, and she had good legs. All she needed was a little TLC. He didn't want a lot of money for her as he had only bought her for a wedge. Apparently when a box car of horses are loaded, if there isn't enough room for one more horse they will stick a pony in. The thinking was the tighter they were packed the less rocking and chafing of the hide as they made the long trip from the West.

We practically lived with the pony that summer. She received lots of carrots and cookies. Pretty soon her coat was shiny and black and her step livened up. We would take turns riding on her back whenever we had an older person to take her by the head. The next summer we learned to ride by ourselves, under supervision. Whenever the pony got tired of us she would buck us over her head onto the ground. We were tough then, and would hold onto the rein. "Get right back on again." was what every rider knew had to be done. "Show her who's the boss." After a while we learned to stay on the saddle in spite of her bucking. It added to the sport and we would only laugh at her. Learning to ride a horse is something like learning to ride a bicycle, or how to swim, something you never forget. I was glad I learned while I was young, from a pony, less distance to the ground.

Some of our older friends from school would visit and insist on riding our pony. In spite of our warnings about the bucking they still wanted to go for a ride. The ride would be short-lived because as soon as they kicked the pony in her sides the pony would break into a gallop and then stop suddenly with her head down and the young lad would go flying over her head. There would be lots of hoots of laughter from the rest of us watching.

Pretty soon one pony wasn't enough for the two young boys, lots of arguments about whose turn it was and who was getting more time than the other. Father settled the argument by adding another horse for my older brother, who would soon be too big for the pony anyway. We spent a lot of happy hours together racing over the fields and going for trail rides in the woods. As we got older we sometimes used the horses to cultivate the garden or haul some firewood to the cellar window.

We didn't have much time for horses once we started high school. There were too many other things to do like homework, household chores like milking the cows or filling the woodbox. In the summer vacation we often worked at the pole yard. Sometimes we would drive a horse; yarding poles from the stockyard to a flat car to be shipped as telephone poles. That wasn't a very nice job as the horse had to be steered with long rope reins, and one had to continuously jump out of the way of the pole rolling back and forth as it was being dragged along.

Around this time we graduated from bicycles and pony to a half-ton truck. The pony lived the rest of her life on the farm giving rides to young family members. She was thirty-five when she passed away and was buried in her favorite pasture. However, we always kept a work horse on the farm to cultivate the garden, rake hay or haul wood.

There was a time I had nothing to do with horses, about twelve years I would guess. Horses take time and all my time was devoted to establishing a business. I was working on construction at both of our local pulp mills. During this time I got married and bought the Homestead from my parents.

Mary and I were settled in on the farm with our young family of three little girls when my sister and her husband made us a gift of a beautiful little pony. It was a package deal of pony harness and jogging cart. Since the oldest was only about five when we received the gift I spent a lot of time driving the cart. A few years later all three could ride but they were too small to let go on their own. I did a lot of jogging then, just to be able to catch hold of the pony if need be. They needed someone to ride with them, I reasoned with my wife. I finally got my first horse, it was very kind and tame; even my oldest daughter could ride him.

As the three young girls became responsible riders they wanted their own horse. I had to give up my steed to my eldest and purchase another pony for the youngest. They were not content just with having horses, they wanted to compete. They also read every horse book and had to see every horse movie. We joined the Miramichi Saddle Club, a group of about fifteen families of horse loving people. The monthly meetings were fondly looked forward to.

The Saddle Club organized horse shows for their own and participated in other horse clubs also. In fact, there was a horse show every other week if one wanted to attend. In the winter tine the monthly meetings continued. We met at different members houses and we had guest speakers, sometimes we would hire an instructor to put on a clinic for a few days. We could all benefit on proper horse training. If we couldn't train them ourselves; there were trainers available for hire. There was no sense going to competitions if you weren't ready.

One can learn a lot by watching a horse show. The judge is

always someone from out of town so they are impartial to the competitors. A good show generally has eight or ten classes. It may start off with halter classes, one for juniors, fifteen and under and seniors, over fifteen. The competitors would lead their horses into the ring and the judge would tell the ring master to walk. He would announce over the P.A. System to walk on the rail. "The rail" means along the fence or boards. The showmen would have numbers pinned to their back and would try to make them visible to the judge. Next the ringmaster might tell them to reverse direction or trot or halt. If any competitor had trouble with their horse; they were "expensed" eliminated from the class. Then the commands became more difficult like, take ten steps back and finally the survivors would be commanded to line up and face the judge who would walk around each horse, look them all over and then ask the show person to pick up its front foot. The best horse and rider always win. This is a person who will be in the top contenders all through the day. To someone watching line classes or trial classes for the first time this could be very boring. Once you understand what these classes are about you can soon tell who have been doing their homework. There are always some new riders and horses showing up and everyone watches to see how good they are.

The latter half of the show is made of games, barrel bending, sack race, bare back riding or egg and spoon racing. This is fun for those whose horses are not disciplined and are sort of red-necked riders. Once my kids mastered the local shows, coming home with high point horse or pony, they wanted to enter the provincial shows, larger and better.

If you are going to compete in the big shows you need to be noticed. Now you are competing with money people who own five thousand dollar horses and twenty-five hundred dollar saddles, they have purebred registered horses and silver plated saddle and bridles. If your horse won't do something you need to do you have to send him to a special trainer to get the kinks worked out. When you're in Rome you do as the Romans do. I had to buy a new horse trailer to transport them to the far away shows at least once a month.

The girls generally came home with one or two first place ribbons, but it was the high point horse they were after. After a while they had so many ribbons and trophies that I was hoping they would get an envelope with money or couple bags of feed. We traded some horses and bought some more silver to add to the saddles but still no high point horse on the provincial circuit, after all they were competing with full time horse trainers and kids that had personal trainers.

My two oldest daughters decided to go to Agriculture college in Truro. Part of the reasoning, I think, was because there was a boarding stable and they would take their horses with them. I kind of went along with the idea as I thought they might spend their time with horses instead of boys. One received an Agriculture Technician degree, whatever that is. The other went on to become a veterinarian. The youngest girl took a legal secretary course. Well, I was wrong about the girls spending all their spare time with their horses as both married boys they met at Agriculture College.

There were a few years we didn't have any horses in the barn. But now, there are six horses here, they belong to Karla, my youngest daughter, and her husband and daughter. Paula, the oldest, lives in P.E.I. and they have three kids and two ponies. Krista the Vet lives in St. Stephen and she has two horses. What goes around comes around, I feel sorry for them; it must be in their genes.

March, 2007

THE HUNGRY NINE

We had a ball team right here in Bryenton one time. They used to play in Hubbard's field. I have a vivid recollection of standing on the outside of the page wire fence watching the game. There was quite a crowd gathered, cars parked along the side of the road. We had front row seats right behind first base. Most of us sat in the grass with the daisies and buttercups, the better seats, the granite boulders, were all taken before we got there. We knew a few of the players on our side, and were there to cheer them on and to boo and call insults to the opposition.

They even had a backstop; it was there in the corner of the field, just below Willis's store and canteen. Only chicken wire and fishnet, hanging on four rough posts, but it stopped many a stray ball. Most of the crowd hung out here as they had a chance to mingle with the players in between innings. Those that had money would frequent the canteen next door. Those were the days when you could get a tall bottle of orange crush for ten cents. If you took small sips you could make it last for the whole game. One might treat their best friend to one tiny sip, but just one.

The field was quite level, the best in the community for the softball team, no such thing as hitting the ball out of the park unless it went foul to the right. If so, there were enough kids lined up along the fence to quickly retrieve it and throw it back to the players. The grass was always well groomed. No time out for "lost ball" like some ball fields of the day. "Daisy," the long horned ayrshire and "Betsy," the jersey, their calves and "Champ," the old grey horse did a wonderful job of keeping the grass under control. The animals would be chased back to the rear of the field for game time, well out of harms way. A little time with a rake and shovel would look after the cow paddies in the immediate diamond.

The parking lots were quite convenient, vehicles parked in

the lane that ran to the railroad; it was between Willis's store and Hubbard's field. The further it ran back, the more it became enclosed with alder bushes. Kids were warned to keep clear of the area. The rough crowd hang out back there drinking liquor or mixing those little lemon bottles with their orange crush. Lots of parking, on the side of the highway; with a good view. Although, you would be facing the sun, on those long summer evenings. But the road was higher than the field and one could see over the by-standers lined along the fence, from the comfort of their car. The police didn't mind the parking and would only stop to enjoy the game themselves.

The team was made up of local men, some of them just returned from overseas. These vets were in prime shape and enjoyed the comradeship which they had become accustomed to. The other half were locals who were younger or older, but they had to be good to make the team. They were serious about their game and played to win. As their fame spread, cars from the nearby communities would take up space along the highway at game time. No admission was ever charged, but quite often, about the middle of the game, a couple of young lads would "pass the hat," and anyone who could would throw in a little to help with the expenses, for balls and bats or a little gas for travelling. Some of the players didn't have jobs, or money, but in summer ball was the most important thing, anything else was second best.

In the spring, in Bryenton, a young girl's fancy would turn to love, but a young man's fancy was "ball." If they wanted any attention the place was at the game. So the girls dressed up, combed and tied ribbons in their hair, put their lipstick on and pulled their short sleeve sweater as tight as they could. Then they would take up their place between the opposing teams. This was so they could get attention from both sides. Sometimes they would meet new boys from the opposing team and would even be known to talk to them a little. But this was frowned upon by the "loyal locals," who always saw them as the "bad guys."

Not many players had cars but transportation was no problem as they always had the truck at their disposal. Elmer Bell, an oversized middle aged, cigarette smoking and the most kind hearted man in the neighbourhood, owned a truck. He thought of the team as his own and would finish his wood deliveries early in the day to cater to the team. He could haul 40 - 50 on the back with the four foot sideboards on, and three to five in the cab. And so, players and fans would meet at the ball field to catch the truck if they were the visiting team. They didn't have to travel far as they played only the nearby communities of Quarryville, the Navy Depot, and Blackville. The Navy Depot had the best field; it was properly graded and well equipped. It was built with Federal money to entertain the workers who worked there and lived in the long row of houses on the property.

No team sported uniforms in those days, not that they wouldn't like to, but uniforms cost a lot of money. There wasn't any business in the area to sponsor uniforms like they had in Newcastle or Chatham; anyway they were out of their league. At first, they didn't even have a proper name, just "the Bryenton team." Other teams had names like "Tigers," "Braves," or "Lumber Kings." Whoever named the Bryenton team is unknown; it may have be themselves, the opposition, or some of the non-sports minded people from the area. However, they became known as "The Hungry Nine."

The Hungry Nine defended their name with pride, the same way some of their team defended their flag overseas only a few years before. They would claim that their name came from their desire to eat up their opposition. They thought "their very name," intimidated the other team. However, the opposition would take the stand that when the game was over they would be going home hungry. Those in the neighbourhood who had no use for sports, like my father or the local storekeeper Albert, whose grandson Earl, was one of the nine, claimed they were hungry because they played ball all summer. There were lots of other things they could be doing for the betterment of their families. They could grow a garden, raise some live-stock, do a little haying and everyone could cut wood. Needless to say I was never encouraged in sports or to take in the games like most of my friends. However, I remember having attended a few games in Hubbard's field and they were the highlight of the summer.

I remember one game in particular; the Hungry Nine were hosting the "Dry Sailors," from the Renous Naval Depot. It was going to be a tough one as Renous had beaten them the last time they met. They met early to do a little practice and get ready for them. Elmer was giving them a little pep talk before the game.

"Now lads, keep your mind on the game, I know you can beat them. Those fancy white and blue uniforms don't make them one bit better. That pitcher of theirs, "Cummings," I think is his name, follows a pattern of one strike and then a ball, don't swing at everything. And Earl, you and Sterling should play outfield so the girls won't distract you. Now go out there and give it your best, there is going to be a big crowd tonight, show them what the Hungry Nine can do."

The players have a little more warm-up to do and start throwing the ball with more vigor, their spirits uplifted by the little speech. Eddie, the third baseman, a big rugged man who had a habit of standing on the baseline to prevent a runner from tagging his base, went across the field with shovel and rake. Nothing strange about that; just going to remove a cow-paddy or rake smooth, a little sand around the base. No one noticed him rake the fresh paddy beside the base and cover it lightly with sand. There will be a little green on those white and blue uniforms tonight if they try to take my base, he thought. He was still sore about the beating they received last week and those nice new uniforms that they surprised them with made him a little bit envious.

Finally the game begins the visitors at plate and the Hungry Nine in the field. Charlie is starting pitcher, Randy is on first, Parker is shortstop on right and Toad on second, Francis is short on left and Eddie is third. Eldon is catching and Earl and Sterling are outfield, as Elmer suggested. The game moves fast with no score in the first three innings. The Sailors take the lead with one in the fourth and it is a sea-saw up to the end of the seventh with a score of 3 to 2 with the Sailors still ahead.

Elmer rallies his team and exchanges his pitcher with the shortstop Parker. That should throw them off a little. Parker is a leftie and they couldn't get a hit off him, while the home team even it up at three all for the end of the eighth. The visitors lead off the ninth with a second base hit, their next batter strikes out and another strikes to right short who firsts for a second out. The runner on second moves for third. Strange, this time Eddie doesn't stand in the baseline as he makes a dive for the base. He is safe on base, but when he stands up he is covered in a green sticky mess. Eddie is bent over laughing and the runner is fighting mad, but Eddie is much larger and stronger than him. Eddie protests he didn't know it was there. This threw them completely off their game and the next batter fanned. Then the Hungry Nine led off with Earl getting a two base hit, and then Sterling brought him home with a 4 to 3 over the Sailors. As they were picking up their gear to leave, Eddie suggested they should have bought white and green as the colours blended better on them.

Elmer gave then a little talking to on manners and respect for other teams, but he had a hard time to keep a sober face. If they treat their visitors like that, they could expect the same treatment. Indeed this happened to them the next week after beating the Braves in Quarryville. As the team left the ball field by the Quarry, they were all seated on the back of the truck moving slow and cautiously through the underpass when some poor losers, on the railroad track up above, emptied the fire barrel directly on them.

The Hungry Nine was on a roll that summer and were coming up to the final playoff with Blackville. Quarryville was eliminated by them and the Renous Sailors by Blackville. The team felt it was necessary to do a little practice on Sunday. Now when Hubbard offered the field he told them they could have it for anytime except Sunday. He was a staunch Presbyterian and he believed Sunday was a day of rest.

On seeing the crowd starting to gather in his field he went out to remind them of their agreement. Some of the team were apologetic but others thought they should be allowed to practice, it wasn't doing any harm. He might have forgiven them if the team hadn't called him a crazy old geezer, and a mean old man. Well, that did it, the next day they found their backstop taken down and placed outside the pasture fence, along with their bases.

Since Renous was already eliminated they offered their facilities to the Hungry Nine for the rest of the season, with their sincere hopes that they would beat the team that beat them. It was not so, as Blackville beat them in four straight. The team kind of fell apart since that next year some quit playing and some went with other teams. But I'll never forget the surprised look on the face of that Sailor with the green and white and blue uniform.

JESSIE

Every time I go into our living room, I remember Aunt Jessie. The large beautiful Christmas cactus sitting in the corner seems to welcome me; the same feeling I got when I visited her. Her Cactus seems to like it here, it sits on a small table in the corner as it doesn't like too much light. It hangs down around its pot and is a lustrous green. There are a few florescent pink flowers spaced evenly around the plant. We didn't notice the buds on it until a few days before Christmas. In fact we were beginning to wonder if it would like its new home.

How old the plant is, I do not know, but I remember it was always there with her in her "knitting room," as she called it. My wife, Sylvia, says it was there the first time she visited and we have been married for forty years. Every time we visited we always had to admire the Cactus and check for buds. Will it blossom at Christmas time, Valentines or Easter, was the question. Jessie had other plants also, but this was the predominate one in the winter months as that was the only time it blossomed, and it blossomed profusely.

Aunt Jessie lived alone for the last thirty years or so in a big house in Nelson. It was close to the road and the river was on the other side. In the summer time she spent a lot of her time sitting on her verandah enjoying the view of the river. There was always some activity, as boats travelled back and forth from Ritchie Wharf to Beaubears Island, just up the river a little from her place. Neighbours often stopped by to chat for a while. It was a different story in the winter, she still had a great view of the river from the front room, but there was always a cold cutting wind off the wide expanse of the river.

Although Nelson, is a cold spot in the winter, I never remember her house being cool. It was about eighty, Fahrenheit, in the kitchen and only a little cooler in the other rooms. Her house was always clean and tidy and so was she. Always cheerful and busy on a pair of socks or mittens, which she would give away. Her's wasn't the heavy rough wool socks, like most hand knitted ones. You could wear the ones she knitted in a pair of dress shoes. They were made with fine yarn and closely knit. I have a pair in my dresser yet, I don't wear them anymore. I don't want to wear a hole in them.

Whenever we visited her the first thing she did was to put the kettle on. You just had to have a cup of tea and a Scotch cookie with white frosting and a piece of red cherry on top. If it was near the Christmas season she would get me to try her fruitcake. She didn't have to coax me any as I always thought she made the best dark fruitcake. "I know you like a cup and saucer," she would remark, "me too" she would say. "It makes the tea taste better," she added as she passed me a gold gilded flower patterned China cup and saucer. As we munched cookies and tea she listened to our kids tell of their achievements. She always inquired about their horses. She had a fondness for horses as there were always horses in their barn when she was young. In fact she and her sisters often visited other friends ten or twenty miles from home by sleigh or wagon. She would laugh as she told us stories about a horse running away on them and her new Easter bonnet blowing off on the Morrissey Bridge.

Jessie was the youngest of her family of five girls and one boy. Her father was a blacksmith and her mother a school teacher before she was married. Jessie's sisters received a good education, got married and moved away. As was the case in those days the youngest one stays home and looks after her aged parents. In return they inherit the homestead. Jessie had no regrets, she had a happy childhood, but she added she was well accustomed to hand me down clothes when she was going to school. She graduated from school with a secretarial degree. She was a bookkeeper at

O'Brien's Store, a nearby general store. After the pulp mill was built in Nelson she became the payroll accountant there, until she retired.

While working at the pulp mill she met and married Freeman Johnston from Red Bank. By this time she was past the child bearing age, so they had no children of their own. But, loving children; they took great interest in the neighbours kids. She would talk about them and speak of their achievements as if they were her own. Of course nieces and nephews were treated with great fondness.

This kindness returned to her years later when her husband died in his early sixties. She found herself alone again. She had a car but never learnt to drive. The neighbours comforted her and did little chores like shopping, picking up her groceries and driving her wherever she wanted to go. Being independent like she was, she got a neighbour to teach her to drive. On her ninetieth birthday she drove to Chatham and back by herself to pick up her groceries. She laughingly told us about it, she said she had a little habit of turning the wheel a little in the direction she was looking. A policeman held her up on her return trip. She showed her license and registration and he bade her to keep on. "We were only checking for drinking drivers and you seemed to be wandering a little," he explained. "Did you tell him you were celebrating your birthday?" I asked. "Heavens no, he would have thought I was drinking for sure."

As she grew older her family grew bigger. The kids she once befriended, now had children of their own and Aunt Jessie's was their favorite place to visit. She always had a cookie or piece of fudge for a little one. She refused to admit she was old; in fact she was never ready to join the local senior citizens club. "Maybe when I get a little older," she would say with a little chuckle. Her last four years were pretty rough; she was in and out of the hospital with pneumonia several times. Then she had a bout of cancer and had to spend a couple of months taking treatment. She bounced back, with encouragement from all who knew her. Nieces and nephews helped her as well as many non-relatives from the community. However, in her ninety-second year she had another breakout with cancer as well as that old pneumonia and she gave up.

The funeral was held at the United church in Nelson on June 30th, 2008. It was a large funeral with Rev. Wiseman and her longtime friend Rev. Feltmate assisting. After the service the trustees of her will, brother John and cousin Burt, handed each of her heirs an envelope. It stated that Aunt Jessie had bequeathed each of us a designated gift. We decided to meet at her house on Saturday, two weeks later.

As planned we all came prepared to pick up her lifetime accumulation. The house had to be cleaned out as it would be going up for sale with the proceeds to be fairly divided. Jessie had the designated pieces labeled with a name on masking tape stuck on the bottom of the piece. Everyone was busy packing dishes and furniture and antiques. I got quite a truck load myself, including two chairs. She had told someone she was leaving me the lazy boy chair because I always seemed to enjoy it whenever I visited. At the end of the day there wasn't much left, the house looked pretty bare. Sitting at the head of the stairs were these two old Christmas cacti, one bigger than the other. They both looked pretty bedraggled as they, like Aunt Jessie, went through a hard time while she was sick.

By this time all cars and trucks were pretty well packed. "What about her plants," someone asked? Everyone agreed that we should take the cactus, dusty and dried out as it was. On the way home Sylvia told me she hoped the cactus would rejuvenate as she remembered it years ago. When we unloaded she insisted that we leave it outside in the shade of the maple tree. I questioned if it would be okay outside as it was probably never outside before. "My mother always kept hers that way," she replied. "However," she added, "I think the pot is too small."

We found a larger pot and I got some good plant soil and replanted it. Now and then Sylvia would give it a little watering with liquid fertilizer added. It looked pretty good by the time we moved it in before frost time. It looks just great now and unlike the chairs and dishes, we have a living memory of Aunt Jessie. We miss the little visits with her and we also miss the little visits we would receive from my two sisters, Joyce and Emily as they tried to see her once a month or so. Cousin Burt says he feels the same as not only does he miss his regular visits with Aunt Jessie, but his two sisters also from Fredericton don't come over very often anymore. We laugh that we even think of her every time we have Chinese as Aunt Jessie used to love to go out for Chinese. We all have happy memories and mementos, and I; I have a cactus we call "Jessie" blooming in my living room.

JOHN DEERE GREEN

Now a Cadillac is a nice car, a prestigious car. So is a Lincoln or Mercedes Benz. Farmers don't care much for fancy cars as long as they have an old half ton to get them around. Their tractor is a different story, it is their work horse. A farmer is judged by his tractor. You can tell if he is prosperous or not as you drive by his place. They always have a habit of parking their machinery all around the yard, and visible to the highway.

As you drive through the country you notice some farms with various pieces of machinery sitting around. If, they are parked helter skelter and rusty; that tells you something. Not a very prosperous farmer, that. Another farmer may have newer equipment, newer paint, not so rusty. He is either doing better or has a larger mortgage. Now the number of tractors is important too. If more than two it must be a good sized farm. That farmer must have hired help; one glance will tell you that.

The colors tell you something too. Most of the farms have various colored machinery. That means they are pretty shrewd, they shop around a lot. They have no allegiance to any one dealer; they just want the most for their money. Who can blame them, but there is one catch. The machinery dealers don't take them seriously as they try for service. In their quest for the best price they often buy inferior machinery that doesn't hold up. As far as the dealer is concerned; too bad. He haggled the price down to rock bottom; there is nothing left for service. They would just as soon if he would take his business elsewhere.

When you see a solid color lineup you can be sure that is a contented farmer. He knows his machinery and has a good working relationship with his dealer. Obviously he has been farming for some time to accumulate such a line. He must be prosperous as he hasn't mixed machinery to save on the price.

This is the kind of customer the dealer appreciates; they want to keep him happy. When this farmer wants something, they bend over backwards to service his machines.

Now there are a lot of different kinds of tractors. Some are American built and some are European or Japanese. Each one has their own identifiable color. The old American built tractors had solid colors. Massey Harris was a bright red, International was a beet red, Ford was a dark blue and John Deere was a dark green. Many of the foreign models have pastel shades. They are seriously trying to enter the American market by undercutting the price range for a comparative American model with the same horse power. This is still a hard sell as most of the dealers are new in the farm machinery business. The failure rate is quite high; if they don't sell enough tractors they will likely fold and where, will the farmer, get service for his European machine then.

The older farmers have another reason, besides service, that they are quick to point out. As I have often heard them say that they fought against those so and so's in the war and they certainly wouldn't want any of their machinery on their farms. Not that they are still farming now but most of their sons have been warned.

I have driven across the country a few times now. It has been my observation that the most prosperous farms have a big green tractor with yellow wheel rims. The more prosperous; the more John Deeres. The larger the farms; the larger the tractors. Out West they grow real big, they are two stories high with dual wheels front and rear. The driver sits up in an air conditioned cab and listens to music as he farms the prairie.

Now would someone give me a kick in the ass, as I painfully remember what I gave up without giving it a chance. You see my brother and I once owned the John Deere dealership in this area. We started off pretty good as we sold a dozen new tractors the first year. After a while we had most of our capital tied up in old tractors – the trade-ins. No one wanted those old dogs at any price.

We finally became discouraged as our new tractors escalated out of the price range. As I recall our Canadian dollar dropped to a new low and since John Deere was manufactured in the Southern States our tractors suddenly became forty percent higher than Massey or International. Only a very wealthy farmer could afford the superior John Deere. I had to give up my salesman job and start working with my hands. Eventually we gave up the dealership and took up other occupations.

Not too long after the John Deere Co. cut their basic price when they realized some farmers were switching their allegiance because of the price. They even built a few manufacturing plants in Ontario to compete with Canadian tractor companies. The dealers who were able to withstand the drought have grown and are doing very well. John Deere supplied their dealers with all kinds of promotional material. We handed out calendars, pens and John Deere caps to customers.

One of the big promotions was "John Deere Day." It was generally held about the end of February when the days started to lengthen and the farmers started to think of spring. Our area supervisor, Mr. Frank, always assisted us with that one. It required quite a bit of preparation but was worth every cent it cost. This was how we found out what piece of machinery the farmer was longing for, to add to his lineup.

We used to rent the United Church hall and mail out invitations to every farmer in the area. The form letter encouraged them to bring the whole family for an evening of movies and entertainment. There were door prizes like irons, electric kettles, and alarm clocks. If that didn't do the trick there were a few John Deere toy tractors that might appeal to their kids.

Kids were allowed to stay up late that night to spend a

night on the town. For some it was the only time the whole family went out together except for the odd church service. The hall would be full of farmers and their kids; it was like the annual farmers get together. Some of the town kids would slip in also. They were lured by the advertisement promising comedy movies, refreshments and donuts.

Everyone was given a card to fill out in order to qualify for the door prizes. They were to fill out their name and check off whatever piece of machinery they were interested in from the list below. There was a list of the different models of tractors. Also, a list of planting and harvesting equipment. The third list contained manure spreaders, lime spreaders and haying equipment. Practically every piece of equipment that John Deere made was there. After the farmer checked off what he would like to have sometime he deposited the card in the ballot box.

Within a few short weeks the company would mail out specific literature on the machinery they had checked off. We also kept a record of their want list and it was my job to follow up on the tips. I had to try to get them to sign on the dotted line. If he didn't have the cash, no problem, we had an easy payment plan. We didn't have to worry about non-payment, all farmers were honest.

There would be a loud round of applause as Abbott and Costello came on the movie screen set up on the stage. Mr. Frank ran the projector so he alternated comedy film with farming pictures featuring the newest of the John Deere line. After about an hour of this there would be a refreshment break. We would mingle with the farmers as they helped themselves to the coffee and donuts. The young lads helped themselves to chocolate milk or fruit juices.

Fifteen minutes later everyone would take their seat for the next movie featuring the "Little Rascals" or the "Three

Stooges."

"Now we have to get ready for the draw," Mr. Frank said to me after he got the projector off and running.

"Come on into the back room with me, we have work to do."

He shut the door behind us and took the big ballot box and emptied it out on a table.

Up till that point I always thought a ballot box was secret. To alter it in any way was illegal, sort of like jury tampering, or something like that.

"Now we separate the sheep from the goats," he chuckled. "The farmers and any of their family, that you are sure of, go back in the box, the rest go in the garbage bag here." Since I knew most of the farm surnames it was up to me to make the decision. The visitors from town automatically were deposited into the garbage bag. He left me to it as he went out to supervise the projector.

The evening ended up with the draw, the hot items went first. Then he announced we would draw a few more complimentary prizes, John Deere caps. Every farm family had some winnings to take home. The town kids only received a little entertainment and a lunch, so everyone went home happy.

I am amused when I go to farm shows and there is a ballot box sitting on the corner of their booth. There is always a crowd going around stuffing these boxes in hopes of winning a free television. You might find an old salesman standing back thinking of years gone by and admiring the new line of John Deere green.

JUST A DREAM

I am sitting up in the recreation room playing checkers. Thank God for checkers, the only thing that hasn't changed over all these years. There are quite a few out today, about 50, and the sun is shining. Guess I shouldn't complain, we are pretty well looked after. We have a comfortable place to stay and we should be happy, but look around, do you see any happy people?

Today is Day 136; we began at 6 o'clock-first bell. That is the time we men have to get up, we all have to walk down the corridor in our blue plastic shorts to the shower room. We have one half-hour to walk through the shower tunnel and to shave. It is kind of humiliating at first, to see all these used up old bodies stripped down to just a little plastic short, and of course the ever important tag hanging around our necks with our social insurance number on it.

We use the tag for everything; every room has a slot that we have to insert, to record our entrance. That is so we can be followed by computer. When we go for lunch we insert it into the machine to get our provisions. The machine knows how much to serve, according to our required weight and prescribed diet.

At 7 o'clock we men go to the cafeteria, we pick up our bowl and mug and proceed to the machine. First we place the mug and bowl in the proper place; then insert our plastic card, and we receive our required portion.

You don't have to worry about false teeth here; everything goes through the blender and is served in a bowl. We eat our mush, and guess what we are eating, but no one really knows. We are told it is the proper food for us, full of nourishment and vitamins.

At 7:30 we return to our rooms, and the ladies take over the cafeteria.

At 8:30 we have to go for our exercise. We all have to

participate, if we want to stay here. Those who don't co-operate are shipped out, and are never heard of again, we call it "never land." The exercise isn't too bad, 15 minutes of stepping and bending. Most of us are in pretty good shape after being here a few years. The newcomers are usually overweight and it takes them a little time to adjust.

At 9:30 it is Chapel time for those interested, I go most days, except for the days those pagan religions have service; they demand and receive equal time.

Most of us go to Chapel when the Christian denominations have service; at least it gives us hope of a better place. Hope is what we desperately need, those poor pagan religions talk about being re-incarnated as a cow or a cat,-not too much to look forward to there.

At 10, those of us who have a spouse are allowed to visit. I was down to Mary's room for a few minutes, but she wasn't in a very good mood so that is why I am here playing checkers with Bob.

Bob is not too bad a checker player; I let him win now and then. Mostly we just talk about old times. Such a nice day today, just like a day one would like to go fishing or do a little work around the yard. Those days are all behind us now, we lament.

"How long have you been in here Tom?" asks Bob.

"Four years now,-came in when I was 64."

"How come?"

"Well the last few years I couldn't get a job anywhere. We hung out as long as we could, didn't have much money laid away, and the government took my place for taxes. How about you?"

"Two years. I was lucky, I worked till I was 65, and I thought my government pension was going to look after us then, but they cancelled the pension, in favour of this place. It makes me so angry, but what can we do?"

"Don't know. One consolation- we are all equal here, no one has anything of their own."

"That's for sure," says Bob," not even the clothes on our backs. I get so tired of these blue outfits all the time."

"Well you don't have to go through your closet trying to decide what to wear everyday," says Tom. "Too bad the politicians wouldn't spend a few days here; see how they like the great system."

"Those fat cats-you know what a politician is Tom."

"No. What?"

"They are just an ordinary man with a big mouth and no conscience."

"That's right!"

"I was watching the news last night, and I see where our Premier is going to Ontario in June to receive an honorary degree at York University. They have great things to say about him, all he is doing for his province, bringing down the debt, making work and taking care of the elderly, the homeless and the helpless."

"Yes, they say he is setting an example for the rest of Canada-heaven forbid!"

"They are good at making themselves look good. We wouldn't have this debt if they hadn't created it buying votes."

"Yes, well now they don't have to buy anymore. My nephew told me he witnessed all the red shirts, and the blue shirts, having the best of a time the other night at the yacht club, - thicker than thieves!"

"And why wouldn't they, after giving themselves a big raise, pretty smart of them to give the blue shirts the same amount. Why upset the apple cart? So they go along with everything."

"Whatever happened to the good old days, the 80's? The 90's weren't too bad either."

"You know the government handed over our Crown land to a couple of large companies to do as they see fit. They gave them stumpage and tax breaks, and even let the companies do their own scaling. Then they helped themselves to the pension funds."

"They were so concerned with big business they lost touch with the people. Now they are taking everyone's property for taxes, because they don't have jobs. The large corporations are having a field day, buying up private land. The rich are getting richer and the poor are getting poorer. There are hardly any middle class people left."

"There is no stopping them, they intimidated the daily papers; did you notice they don't publish letters to the editor anymore?"

"You know the Premier's friend, who is in the recycling business; he got a big grant to build a blast furnace. Well, that furnace is supposed to burn hazardous waste. What else do you think they are burning?"

"No!"

"Oh yes! Don't get down and useless or you will be going out in that big ambulance. To the hospital they say, but I never see anyone come back, have you?"

"Kind of a poor survival rate, wouldn't you say?"

"If you don't have any visitors for months, you might end up there sooner. Save the government a pile of money, wouldn't it?"

"There is the 11:00 o'clock bell, time for mush again!"

"See you after the movie this afternoon."

"Yeah - We should plan an escape!"

They meet again at 14:00 hours.

"Were you serious about breaking out?" Bob asks.

"Yes, do you think we could pull it off?"

"Not much to lose if we don't."

"Let's see," says Tom, always looking for a challenge. "But what about Mary?"

"Oh she will never miss you anyway, will she?"

"No. I don't suppose so," Tom replies.

"Settled then, let's see, we will need some clothes, street

clothes, money and a car."

"And a gun," says Tom.

"No! No violence or I'm out."

"O.k., but how do we do it?"

"Very carefully; we will watch for a couple of new men to come, then we will steal their street clothes out of the utility room."

"O.k., next we will need money. Can we con our kin for a few hundred?"

"How will we do that? I know, let's tell them we have picked out our tombstone and the agent wants money."

"Yes! How could they refuse?"

"And a car," asks Tom.

"Well, we will have to borrow one from the orderlies. You know that new guy; I bet he leaves his keys in his jacket pocket. He is always jingling them when he comes in. He hangs it in the utility room."

"O.k.," says Bob.

"Two weeks time, should we say?"

"Yes, we will try in two weeks."

Two weeks later, last bell at 9:00 o'clock, or 21 hours as they say at the home, the two slip out of the rooms. No one is watching the monitor as the nurse, watchman, and orderly are having a game of cards in the nursing station.

Everything goes as planned; they let themselves out with the orderly's keys and help themselves to his car. A couple of hours later they are on a plane headed for Cuba.

When they arrive at their destination they go to customs and ask for political asylum. They were welcomed by the Cuban journalists who were anxious to report their story. After some consultation the Cuban government granted their wish. They would be required to work 4 hours a day to pay for their stay.

Since Bob was a retired schoolteacher, he was asked to

teach an adult class, mostly female waitresses, how to talk English. Tom, having been a carpenter all his life, was given a crew of eight young men and he was to supervise building self-contained cottages along the beach. They stay together at the hotel where Bob has his classroom, and are treated like royalty.

In the afternoons they sit on the beach and sip the local refreshments. Bob found a few clubs and balls and is practising his putting abilities.

"Not a bad life, eh, Arnold Palmer," says Tom. "Real nice place, real people, real food, and we are still useful."

"Yes," says Bob, "I enjoy my job, those beauties really want to learn."

"My boys are good workers too," replies Tom.

"Did I tell you I got a letter from my nephew yesterday," asks Bob.

"No."

"Well, he said our stories landed up in the Toronto Star, and when our N.B. Premier went to York University to pick up his honorary degree they had to have a police escort to get him out. The students all booed him when he was getting his honour."

"That is good; maybe he will re-think his seniors programme. I was talking to a couple of tourists the other day. They always stop and ask a lot of questions when they see that I am a foreigner. Anyway they say things are still pretty good for seniors in Ontario, if we ever go back that is where we should go."

"Why would we want to leave a place like this," says Bob, lighting up his big Havana cigar. "I know a couple of ladies that would like a little private tutoring, if you know what I mean. How long before one of those cottages will be done?"

"Pretty soon, but remember we never came down here to get shot," says Tom, with a laugh. "Practice your putting, I think I'll take a little nap," sliding his hat down over his face.

LETTER TO SANTA

Dear Santa:

It has been nearly sixty years since I last wrote you asking for a pair of hockey skates. I sure had a good time playing with the older boys on the river ice. The next year my young friends convinced me there is no such thing as Santa Claus. I felt I had lost a good friend.

You might call it second childhood that I write you again today. You see, there is something I have been wishing for. It is called a Tenon tool, they can be found in the Lee Valley Carpentry Tool Catalogue on page fifty-seven. Actually, I would like to have two of them – II-e, is a one and one eighth and II-f is one and a seven eighth.

I have been wishing for this tool ever since we went on that Alaska trip last summer. You see, all the tourist attractions featured home made furniture. There were rest benches, lawn chairs and tables. I could tell they used some kind of a Tenon tool. The legs, rungs and back uprights, were all precision turned, to fit into the drilled framing. The tenon piece of hard peeled alders or black spruce fit the mortise nice and tight so everything stayed solid.

I was fascinated with the rustic outdoor furniture and would like to give my hand a try at it. I told my friends about the furniture and inquired where one might find such a tool. I mistakenly called it a dowelling tool and all the building supply places told me they didn't handle such a thing. Finally, my son-in-law Darren told me his father Doug has volumes of Lee Valley Catalogues; surely they would have one if there is such a thing. He got back to me and gave me a catalogue.

"Look on page fifty-seven, although they don't call it a

dowel tool I am sure it is what you are looking for."

I was excited as I turned to the page. I wondered if he really knew what I was talking about. Sure enough there was a picture of a whole set of Tenon tools. There were half dozen of them in the layout, every size from three quarters to two and a quarter. One can buy them separately or get the whole set for four hundred and twenty-five. They are a little pricey but Lee Valley sells nothing but the best, I realize that.

The one and one-eighth would be good for small stuff like chair rungs and railings and the one and seven-eighths would be good for fence rails and table legs. I guess I could get by with only two of them. The smaller one costs sixty-five dollars and the other is ninety-five. That would only be one hundred sixty-five, plus tax of course.

Now that in itself is quite a bit just to give it a try, not knowing how my handy-work will turn out. But that isn't all, in the write-up about this fine set of tools it mentions that all you need to power this tool is a half-inch electric drill. I have an electric and a cordless but they are both quarter inch. A half inch drill will cost one twenty-five or more. The Makita, one half inch, is the king of them all as far as I am concerned. The DeWalt is a pretty good one too.

Come to think of it I would probably need a couple of Forstners bits to make the holes for the tenoned pieces to fit into. I have spade bits but that large a size wouldn't work in heavy lumber. The Forstners bits cost about forty dollars each. I might be able to find an old draw knife kicking around the shop. A left-over from the days of hand peeled pulp wood or pit-props. I wouldn't want to pay the twenty-five dollars for the nickel plated model in the catalogue.

All in all, the complete package would likely cost four hundred or more, to say nothing about a wood vise. That would be nice to have to put the pieces of wood into while I hand shave it. The hardware in the catalogue is priced at twenty-seven fifty. I guess I couldn't very well do without it. Now we are getting close to four-fifty. Not much chance Mary will go along with that expense for a "bunch of foolish tools that you would only use once or twice, she will say.

"Besides, I don't much care for that old wooden stuff anyway. It looked all right in the Yukon, but you are in a civilized community now. One can buy all the lawn furniture they want at Zellers or Canadian Tire for much less than the tools will cost you, what are you thinking, give your head a shake." I can hear her now.

How can you argue with logic like that, she is probably right? Another point is that we have already bought our Christmas present for each other. We purchased our tickets for a week in Florida around the second week in January. We can't afford any furniture making machinery this year, sorry.

Well, Dear Santa you always came through for me when I believed. You did the same for my kids. And since I am entering second childhood perhaps you might work a little magic in my favor.

Tom

P.S.
I have been a good boy all year.

MARY'S ROAST PAN

"Get me the roast pan out of the basement please," Sylvia asks, as she goes to pluck the turkey out of the kitchen sink. It was defrosting overnight in a sink of water. As I retrieve the big box shaped old roast pan I try to calculate how old it is. One thing for sure, it was well used, before my wife inherited it. I believe Sylvia's mother promised it would be here when she was through with it.

Whenever I see it I remember Mrs. Bell and the big old fashioned turkey dinners she prepared. Mary was a great cook and usually invited all her family for a Sunday dinner. "The more the merrier," she would welcome us in to her already crowded house. "You just go in and join the men, Paul," as I passed through the back kitchen. "And how are my girls today?" she would ask as they all crowded in for a big hug.

There would be a big table set up in the kitchen for the adults and another in the middle for the kids. The men, Mr, Bell, his son, Alvin, and Sydney, I and both sons-in-law, would get comfortable in the dining room. We would talk the weather, our work and the local news. In the kitchen the women were helping prepare the food. They would be laughing as they talked about their young families. The chatter, the laughter and the aroma coming from that small back kitchen was something joyful to remember.

The children would be served first at their table. Then the rest of us would be asked to sit in. The men sat tightly in the back side of the table. Of course the reasoning was that they didn't have to serve anyone. The girls wait out on everyone. After a bulging big meal we generally have the option of a couple different kinds of pie.

As soon as we finished our tea the men folk would retire

to the inner room while the young women cleared the tables and tidied up the kitchen. Then they would come after us to go home. Just in time too; as conversation was generally run out; and some of us were about to doze off. Mary would be at the door begging us to stay a little longer and at least take some of the leftovers with us.

Not only does that oversized, stained and dinged roast pan bring happy memories of Mrs. Bell, it signifies family gatherings. I don't know if Mary ever knew what an uplift it was for our young family to get together every now and then for dinner and conversation. My wife especially needed the break as she was holding a full time job as a nurse as well as looking after our three pre- school aged daughters with very little help.

Even today Sylvia, like her mother before her, is preparing a feast. There is a pot of peeled potatoes, another full of carrots and turnips. A squash sits on the counter as well as a big bowl of dressing. I spot an apple pie on the counter thawing out. "Better put another leaf in the table," she says as she starts to name off who is coming. I count with her that is how many plates and chairs I will have to place.

Like Mary used to say, "The more the merrier." I will have to agree judging by the size of the bird. I'll probably get a chance to pick a few turkey bones tomorrow and then Sylvia will salvage the rest for turkey soup, which she freezes and brings out some cold day.

If our girls would have their choice of Sylvia's pots and pans, I am sure the old roast pan would be first choice. Whoever gets it must be prepared to hold big family dinners because it is too big for one family. A much smaller one could satisfy a small family but just think of what they would be missing.

THE MCKENDRICK LAKE FIRE

"Where's the fire Willie?" I asked, pointing to the smoke billowing up like a cloud on the western horizon.

"Don't know, but she's a dandy, bad day, everything so dry, that wind would make it hard to fight. Up the Renous road I would guess. Where's your father today? Might be on their ground, they have a lot of ground up that way. A good wind for fish though. Caught two salmon this morning, I am going down to check the set now, want to come along?"

"Sure, lets go David," as we skip across the field to join our neighbour. Not long until we are in the flat bottom boat inspecting the set net.

"There's one in there, pass me the scoop net," says Willie.

"Wow, what a beauty - how heavy is he Willie?" David asks.

"About ten pounds I guess," Willie replied.

David and I take turns slinging the feed bag over our backs, with the prize inside. Willie opens the ice house door, places this one with the other two on top of the snow and covers them with wet sawdust.

"See your father is home, let's go and see if he knows where the fire is."

Father is busy on the phone calling some of his camp bosses, asking them to gather up men and be there at daylight tomorrow.

There would be trucks moving bulldozers and supplies up during the night.

As soon as he could get a chance Willie asks "Where is the fire, Earl?"

"Up on the Sullivan grant; just this side of McKendrick Lake. I had been saving that piece for a rainy day, a lovely stand of spruce logs. Hope that wind goes down tonight. I would like to know how it got started."

"Are you going up Dad?" I asked.

"Yes, my boy, first thing in the morning."

"Can David and I go too?" I asked, "We could help fight fire."

"Well I suppose, it is not a nice job though, better get to bed early, as we will have to do the chores before we go in the morning."

"You lads go ahead - I'll milk and feed tomorrow. I'll be around all day - just tending the net and weeding the garden. Had a good day today, Earl, three beauties, two ten pounders and one about fifteen."

"Thanks Willie" and we hit for bed, so excited we had a hard time to get to sleep. "Just think; going to a real fire, hope we can stop that fire."

Next morning Mother fixed breakfast for her three men. It was the usual; oatmeal porridge, topped with brown sugar and milk and a side dish of prunes, toast and jam. All the time she is giving us instructions: "Now be careful, stay with your father, don't get burnt. And Earl, don't let them out of your sight. Don't like the idea of them going to a fire - too young, might get hurt, you look out for them. Do you need a lunch to take with you?"

"No, there will be a cook house set up at the fire. Lets go boys, don't worry Dell, I'll take good care of them."

"Bye Mom and we struck out. First stop Newton's general store to fill up with gas and get a few things at the store.

"We're going to the fire with Dad, we announce as we enter the store."

"Have a good time," says Newton, laughing.

"Give us a scoop of those peppermints there, and a couple of cigars," says Father, laying a bill on the counter. "Oh yes, a couple of bottles of lemon for Pat, he'll be needing some to bake a cake," as he gives Newt a wink.

On our way again, chomping on the peppermints. "I never knew you smoked cigars, Dad."

"I don't, they are for Albert Stewart, the cook."

"Who is Pat," asked David.

"He is the gatekeeper up at McGraw Brook." Soon we came to the end of the settlement, and the end of the pavement. The dirt road was one continuous washboard of holes. We rattled along driving from one side to the other trying to get around the rougher stretches. Not much traffic, but we met a couple of trucks loaded with sawn lumber. What a dust, after the trucks passed, it seemed to just stay hovering over the road, locked in by trees on either side.

"How much further, Dad?"

"Well let's see, about ten miles to the gate and another ten to the fire."

"Twenty miles; I thought it was a lot handier than that by the smoke. Must be an awful big fire."

Pretty soon we arrive at the gate and the gate is down. Mr. Hayes the keeper has some rope and pulleys rigged up so he can open or shut the gate without even going outside. Everyone must stop and sign the register, their name, place of birth and business. When the fire index is high no one is allowed to go travelling or fishing. The only way Mr. Hayes will open the gate is if you are a fire warden or had a travel permit issued from the Dept. of Natural Resources. Most lumber company officials were issued a fire warden pin each year. Father always stuck his into the sun visor of the car. Fire wardens had the same authority as forest rangers if they should catch someone breaking the fire laws. They also helped each other and were the leaders for fire fighting.

We enter the gate house. First time David and I were ever inside; a table, a cot, and a stove. Not much furniture, just a few chairs. Most days Mr.Hayes doesn't have many visitors, but all hell broke loose with the fire that started yesterday. Father wanted to talk to Mr. Hayes so we went inside.

Mr. Hayes was a dead ringer for Gabby Hayes, a side kick of Gene Autry, in the western movies. He loved to talk and made a habit of asking for everyone he knew once one would sign the register. This paid off pretty well, sometimes someone would have a few bottles of beer or a few groceries left over that they would not want to take home after hunting or fishing trip. Most people that knew him made it a point to have something to drop off.

"Well, Earl; quite a fire, eh! These your boys? Going up to give them a hand eh!"

"Hello Pat, here's that cake flavour you ordered," again with a wink.

"The very best Earl, thanks, thanks a lot, won't be getting out for a while I guess, unless we have a big rain. Too bad about the fire."

"What time did the fire start, Pat?"

"About 1:00 p.m. yesterday I guess. They picked up the smoke from the Rocky Brook tower and called down a little after 1:00."

"Was anyone in the area at the time?"

"Three suspicious characters, right here," says Pat, turning the page back to Wednesday morning. "These three said they were going into McKendrick Lake to fix up Mullins Sport Camp. They didn't look like they were going to do much, no bundles or supplies, lots to drink though. Had to let them go, they had a permit from the forestry in Newcastle."

"Where are they now?" Father asked.

"That's the funny thing, they checked out at 12:55, - right here, said they needed some material and they would be back later, but they never came back."

A couple of trucks full of lumber stop and Mr. Hayes pulls the rope to let them through.

"Coulter's are moving their lumber down to the wharf, in a hurry; they are scared the fire might reach them. If that wind comes up like yesterday it could happen," says Mr. Hayes.

"Surely it won't get that far Pat," says Father, "lets go boys."

On up the road a little way David says "I can't imagine Pat baking a cake, he doesn't look too clean - wouldn't want to be eating it." "Me neither," I replied.

Soon we come to the North Branch Renous River. Coulter's big sawmill is not running; only a couple of trucks and someone with a loader loading them. The lumber yard was still half full with lumber. Smoke is settled down in the valley, making a blue haze, and the smell of forest fire is quite prominent.

"The fire must be awful close now," I said.

"Another five miles or more," says Father as we rattle along.

After a few minutes we come to a newly bulldozed road, a bunch of fuel barrels. Obviously this is where unloaded the bulldozer. We follow this new road about two miles then we see the fire camp headquarters.

Here we see about a half acre freshly bulldozed clearing, the other side of the site both up and down all blackened from fire. There are two large tents set up. One is the cook house, and the other is sleeping quarters.

There is a couple of long tables set up, loaded with food. Cases of canned goods are piled up at the end of the table. A cook in white uniform and a couple of young lads with long white aprons are standing around. Men are sitting around everywhere with their tin plates and mugs, some eating and some smoking.

All eyes are turned to us as we enter. Of course they know who Father is as his car has O'Brien Lumber Co., South Nelson printed on the door.

"How come they are not fighting fire Dad?" "Well Son, they have to have a break, they probably have been out since daybreak."

Father parks the car out of the way and we follow him over

to a table where the timekeeper and a couple of forestry officials are standing. Everyone seemed to be looking us up and down. The older men all welcome us, 'Lo Earl, 'Lo Earl as Father exchanges Hello's with them, 'Lo John, 'Lo Lawrence, etc. Bert
Kelly is set up as timekeeper and he has everything under control.

"A couple more men eh, Earl?"

"Yes, these are the best fire fighters there is in Bryenton," he says.

"What are your names?' he asks and enters us on his tally sheet.

"How many men Bert?"

"86 before you came," he replied. "About half are still out, waiting for these lads to spell them off."

"How does it look this morning boys," he inquires of the two uniformed foresters.

"It is about a mile below us with a quarter mile front. The boys are doing good this morning. It got quite a head start on us yesterday." They open some maps up pointing out the areas. David and I stick our heads in under to see what they are talking about. "We estimate about 200 acres lost so far," they explain. It is pretty well contained on three sides.

"Good, I wonder if we can hold her here, at this brook," and he puts his finger on the map. "As I remember there wasn't much lumber right here, it was cut over about ten years ago by Sullivan; should be easy bulldozing. If you can get a couple of bulldozers down there to plough up a fire break."

"Good idea, Earl, we will get right on it. We will go in with Joe, the truck driver, transporting men back and forth to the front. We will take Matchetts and Coulters down and leave the other two to help the crew."

Just then the crew bosses, those with the fire wardens pins on, call out to get aboard, and the crew slowly rise to their feet. The truck heads down towards the front as we head over to the cook house.

"How are you, Albert?" says Father.

"Just great, Earl; quite a fire, eh? Can't blame this one on the lightening, - wouldn't mind a good old fashioned one right now though."

"Hey - you lads got something for Albert haven't you?"

We each pass out a cigar, Albert thanks us and tells us to go ahead and have a lunch. The other crew will be in soon, and he calls out to his cookies to load up the tables before they tackle the dishes.

There is no lack of food at a fire; men have to eat good if they are going to work. Big pans of rolls and tea biscuits; a great big pan, about three feet long, full of sausages; and several pots of beans. There was even a galvanized bucket full of hard boiled eggs, and coffee and tea, cases of juice and canned peaches.

I wasn't very hungry but I couldn't resist a big fat molasses cookie. David went for the do-nuts and Father had a cup of tea and cookie.

"Let's go," says Father, taking his axe in hand, "bring one of those back packs and a shovel." David donned the back pack and I filled it up out of a few buckets nearby. The pack held about five gallons and he had quite a time getting up off his knees. He started off quite wobbly and Father got him to pump about half out on a smouldering log. "Now save some, we might need it."

"But the fire is down that way," I pointed.

"I know, but I want to go across to the lake."

"How far is the lake, Dad?"

"About a mile I reckon."

We went in a westerly direction, up over a hill and then down a long slope to the lake. David and I put out a few small flames that were starting up again, not much real danger though as everything was already burnt. By the time we got to the lake we were about as black as the trees surrounding us.

"We should go for a swim," but Father said "No time for that now." He was looking for something.

"Let's go down here a little," says he as we start to follow the outlet. About one hundred yards down the outlet, there it was, the scene of the crime; a tin can and a frying pan. "Someone had a campfire and it got away, and I bet I know who they were," says Father. There was a little pile of ashes nearby that looked like burnt cloth. Father poked around with his axe and uncovered a buckle. Not a common steel buckle, but a fancy flat brass one. "Look here boys," as he held it up, they must have lost their packsack. He put the buckle in his pocket. The wind off the lake would fan the fire and everything would be out of control pretty fast.

Before we left he blazed a few trees so the spot could be easily found. As we were returning back to camp Father was estimating the loss and that he would have to get someone to cut the larger trees this winter as he couldn't let them go another summer as the worms would be in them. Saw flies lay eggs under dead bark and the next year the eggs hatch and the worms make holes all through the tree making the lumber useless. The small trees would be of no value to anyone.

When we stepped out in the opening, we noticed the crowd was back again for second lunch. They had some new company; O'Brien himself was there with his movie camera. His chauffeur Doug was cranking the machine and Leonard was doing the focusing.
When he saw us he turned the camera in our direction and kept it on us until Father came up to him.

"Hello Earl, thought I would come up and get a few pictures. Here, stand over here in front of these men and I will get one of you on my 35 millimeter." He gets another camera and takes our picture.

"Now tell me about the fire," he insists.

"Well, so far I think we lost about 300 acres, some nice log trees, but I will be able to salvage some. The boys are making a fire break down near McKendrick brook. I think they will be able to head her off there."

"Bet I could get some good shots near the break," says O'Brien.

"Yes, for sure," says Father.

"Hey Joe; got time to run us down to the front?"

"Yes sure and they load the equipment on the back with Doug and father. O'Brien jumps in the front.

"You boys stay here and help Albert, we won't be long."

We had a good time eating and became acquainted with the two cookies. We helped them carry drinking water from the spring nearby. Even if they get the fire contained they would probably stay another week putting out hotspots and picking up fire hoses. They said they like their job and hope they get another fire or two before they have to return to school.

In the meantime Joe returns with the second crew and goes right back with the first crew. Then he returns with Father, O'Brien and Doug.

O'Brien is happy with all his picture taking and he and Doug leave.

"Well, we might as well go too, Boys. I think we have the fire under control. We were quite satisfied to leave also.

On the way home, Father stops at the gate and Mr.Hayes writes down the names and times of the three that were in at McKendrick on Wednesday morning; Also the name of the forester that signed their permit.

"I will be seeing this man in the morning," says Father.

"Politics, that's what it is Earl, politics, friends of someone in politics, think they can come up here and run wild anytime they like, put the power to them Earl."

Don't remember much of the trip home as Father wakes us up at home.

Mother orders us to take off our outer clothes before we come in and to go right upstairs to the bathtub.

Willie rushes right over to get the news of the fire. Father tells him of our discovery and hands him the buckle. He examines it like a diamond.

"Not off a poor man packsack, that's for sure. I guided for Max Stewart last spring and the American sport had a nice leather packsack with a lot of brass buckles on it. Never seen one like it around here, though. Maybe Allen's Sport Shop handles them. They shouldn't let anyone up there when the woods are closed."

Next week the local paper, the North Shore Leader, had headlines; "Arson suspected in McKendrick Lake fire." There was a picture of a crew of fire fighters having a lunch break, and there were a couple of young boys in the picture, but no one could identify them, they all looked like a bunch of coal miners.

"Would you like to go fight fire again boys?" asks Willie. "No," I replied, "I would rather help you fish the net."

TRIP TO ONTARIO

The Preacher was reading the announcements out of the bulletin, and then he threw in an extra one." Would anyone in our Congregation happen to have a half ton that I could borrow for a few days?" He wanted to go back home to pick up a few things he had forgotten to bring when he moved down. Some summer clothes, the kids' bicycles, and they really missed their Bar-B-Q. He was looking right at me, although there were several others with half tons, who could volunteer as well as me.

Since I wasn't working, and we had two vehicles, and no one else offered, I thought it would be the Christian thing to do. So I filled my new truck with gas and took it down to him Tuesday night so he could get an early start the next day. As I handed over the keys I wished him and his wife a good trip and I would get my truck back on Saturday. "But she is not going," he stated "I'll be going alone."

"Well now" I thought. I could use a little vacation myself, and since my truck is going anyway, I should volunteer to help with the driving. He said he would be glad for the company and we could stay at his sisters once we arrived at our destination, Newcastle, Ontario.

Next morning I picked him up; he came out of the manse with a duffle bag, and a case full of tapes. "Oh, oh," I thought, this is going to be a long trip, - all those gospel tapes. We planned our route to cross at St. Stephen, go up through New Hampshire, Vermont and pass through the southern townships of Quebec, then into Ontario. He knew the way well, as he had an old aunt in St.Stephen that he used to visit quite often. Sounds great to me as most would be new country, and I always wanted to see the apple orchard country in the southern townships that I have heard so much about.

Now Sam wasn't a full fledged minister, he was a minister assistant. Our regular minister lived in town and stayed with the town people except for Communion Sunday. Only ordained ministers can administer the sacraments in the Presbyterian Church. But Sam could do the preaching and visiting as well as other minister. He was a good speaker and a good singer. He was about equal to a third year student, according to Presbyterian standards. Apparently he had worked as a bus driver for a while, before entering theology college, and his wife was a secretary and worked as well as raising the three young boys in their family. The family were happily settled in, and Sam's wife was happy to have him share the load of rearing their children.

I had forgotten to mention that Sam also brought a travel cooler with him, which he set up between us. A short distance along the road we bought some pop, juice and ice to keep us fresh along the way. To my surprise he slipped George Jones in the tape deck, next it was Conway Twitty, and he offered me my choice of any Country singer I could think of, as he had them all.

It was a beautiful warm day and we travelled along with the windows down, and the Country music playing. We talked about different things, I couldn't decide if I would rather be a full time farmer or a carpenter, instead of dividing my time between the two. He in turn thought he would like to become a famous evangelist, or a politician.

We reached the border at Calais and had to answer the usual questions: Where are you going, how long will you be staying in the U.S., anything to declare and what is your occupation? Sam said he was a preacher and I said I was a farmer. Gas prices were quite a bit cheaper in Maine so I decided to fill up. Sam looked in the cooler and declared we were nearly out of juice and pop. "What kind would you like Tom," as he headed to replenish the stock. I told him "I didn't think I could drink any more juice, but I do like American beer."

"Me too" he replied and returned with a six pack and a couple of bottles of pop.

"Here Sam, take the wheel, the wife always says I can't drive and gawk around." Sam was a good driver and enjoyed driving and I was enjoying the countryside, beer and music. That night we stayed in a beautiful little place in the hills of New Hampshire. It was almost a ghost town but I guess it would be different during the skiing season as there were ski runs cut in the hills in every direction.

Next morning we passed through New Hampshire and into Vermont. Beautiful country, nice scenery, but the houses looked very humble and the economy seemed to be lagging. All of a sudden we entered Quebec. The eastern townships seemed to be a prosperous looking place - great farming country, apple country with orchard after orchard for miles. Sam was pointing out all the boats, and marinas, the river was actually full of boats, sitting waiting for the weekend.

We stopped to get a little gas and the attendant asked, "Where are you headed?" Sam told him that we are going to cross the Jacques Cartier bridge and on into Ontario. To this he asked if we had heard the news. Well no - we were listening to the tape deck, "Well," he says, "all hell broke loose this morning. The Indians at Oka reserve shot and killed a mountie or two, and they had the road blockaded up ahead. Something about a land claim, they were trying to stop a golf course from being built on one of their sacred burial grounds."

This recent discovery caused us to rethink our route but Sam wasn't familiar with this new road. We thought we would go up the south side of the St.Lawrence and cross at Cornwall. After a couple of hours driving we found ourselves back at the same border crossing into the U.S. that we had passed through earlier in the day. At first we didn't recognize the place; it looked more like a border crossing into Czechoslovakia. There were three State trooper cars on either side of the road and the men were armed with what looked like machine guns. In order to get where we wanted we could detour around the U.S. about an eighty mile drive or we could pass through Vermont again for about twenty miles to the bridge going into Canada. We took the last option, and proceeded very cautiously past the troopers again. Again at the border we were asked the same questions. When they asked my occupation I stated that I was a carpenter.

We finally got to the giant bridge at Cornwall and had to stop at Customs again. The bridge was well guarded, troopers on one side and the military on the other. I guess they were afraid the Iroquois might blow up a bridge. This time when they asked my occupation I stated that I was a farmer. I always have trouble trying to answer the questions. After we were safe on the Canadian side Sam says he really thought that we might be held up and accused of falsifying on our occupation. If they had phoned one of the border crossings to verify our story, they would have found out that I had reported that I was a farmer twice and a carpenter twice. "OK," I says, "when we return we will go back through Canada - all the way!"

Fifty miles past the bridge we finally arrived at Sam's sisters. They lived a few miles back from the super highway between Ottawa and Toronto. The area looked much like our own Miramichi, sparsely scattered houses and lots of trees. As we turned into their yard I noticed a nice house, swimming pool, and in the back yard there was a barn with a corral. Sam introduced me to his sister, a beautiful woman about 35 years old, her husband a heavy man and he looked 10 - 15 years older than her. They had a couple of teenage kids. They showed us our rooms and we had a little talk before turning in.

We learned that her husband had recently been laid off from

his job as an oil company executive. He had been with the company for twenty years and worked in an office in Toronto. He travelled 100 miles each way every day, partly by car pool, and the rest of the way by train - 2 hours each way every day. The company was closing its Toronto office and was moving everything to Calgary. The only other job he could find was to become a transport driver and he was soon going to start, which meant he would be away from home for 5 days at a stretch.

But it was summer holidays now and tomorrow they were going on a trail ride. "Do you ride Tom?" she asked. "Oh yes," I replied, "I am not a great rider but I can stay on, been riding since I was young lad."

"Then it's settled, tomorrow you come with us, we have a spare horse, she is a boarder but her owner doesn't mind us using her. We are going back the old tower road and we are going to meet up with another couple at 9 a.m. It is about three miles each way to the tower."

"Great," I replied, "I was wondering what I would be doing." Sam said he was going to visit his mother and brother and get loaded for the trip back home the next day.

We were around early the next morning and I went with them to get the horses out of the pasture. They each had lovely looking Quarter horses, but the boarder was about as poor a looking horse as I ever saw. She was part Appaloosa as she had some spots. She had poor confirmation, sunken chest and crooked legs, and her ears laid back most of the time.

As I led her to the barn, they asked me to keep her behind as she would kick their horses. We saddled up and walked up the road to meet with the other couple. I had to keep my horse away from all the other horses because of her kicking habit. We all started back the tower road. It was wide enough for two horses but I kept in the middle at the rear. When they came to a nice sandy section they broke into a gallop. I booted my horse to pick up speed to keep up, but with that she pulled enough free rein to get her head down between her legs and after three or four good bucks I landed in the sand in front of her. Still hanging on to the reins I jumped up as quick as possible and I was dusting the sand out of the loose sweater I was wearing. About this time, of course, they looked back to see where I was. They tried to keep from laughing as they inquired if I was hurt. I wasn't hurt any, only my pride, and I often wonder whatever made me say that "I can stay on." I made the rest of the trip alright with that miserable horse, but I kept a tight rein after that. I bet they are still laughing about that poor chap from N.B. whenever they go on a ride.

The next day we started home coming down that big super highway, Sam driving, I wouldn't be able to keep up as everyone was passing each other, and the slowest was about 120 Kms per hour, four lanes each way and more transports than cars. I couldn't but help feel sorry for Sam's poor brother-in-law entering that jungle at his age.

As we were travelling down the busy road Sam related a story to me about the time he was driving bus and run out of fuel right about here.

He was doing some driving for this charter bus company and one morning he got a call to meet their bus at the intersection handy to his home. They had an important delegation of German businessmen who were over here touring some of the pulp mills and had to go to Montreal to catch their plane. Toronto was fogged in or some reason and they had to get to Montreal in a hurry. He volunteered and took off with this nice little compact diesel bus. It was a scenic one with deep windows and was fully air conditioned; all their buses were equipped with phones. He had 16 passengers. About 100 miles down the road the bus began to sputter and he managed to get to the shoulder of the road, before she stopped. He always made sure his buses were full of fuel whenever he took them, but since he was taking over for some one else he never thought to look at the fuel gauge, and it was showing empty. Nothing he could do but to phone back to his company to send out their mechanic with some fuel. The passengers were in an awful way, and encouraged him to try to get it going as they would miss their plane. But there was nothing he could do now, it was out of fuel, he didn't tell them what happened. He just let on he didn't know. The bus started to heat up in the sun without the air conditioner, so he went out and sat in the grass at the side of the ditch. Finally his passengers did the same, they took off their ties and jackets and grumbled amongst themselves and waited for two hours for the mechanic.

When the mechanic arrived he reached in and flipped the switch over to the other tank which was full, and started up the bus. Sam delivered them to Montreal; they had missed their plane by two hours. Needless to say he didn't get any tips that trip.

We crossed the Jacques Cartier bridge in Montreal at the 5 o'clock rush hour. Three lanes going each way and we were in the centre lane. Transports and cars were passing us on both sides. They were blowing their horns and giving us the finger, as Sam was holding to the legal speed limit. The centre lane looks awful narrow when you have a transport passing on either side. I was afraid that they would sandwich us, perhaps it was because of our N.B license plates. This didn't bother Sam as he said they always act like that at rush hour.

That night we stayed in Levis and the next day got an early start and wound our way down the Matapedia valley. The road followed a beautiful clear river, no sign of civilization except for the odd sport camp. I will have to admit that I was glad to get back on home ground, New Brunswick. Even if it wasn't as prosperous looking, as Quebec; at least I knew the language and the people seemed friendlier.

On arrival Sam's boys were on hand to welcome us and they helped us unpack. That is until we unloaded their bicycles; then the three took off up the road for a race. My wife was glad to see me back, but wanted to know why I hadn't called. I replied that she had nothing to worry about as I was in good hands.

That Sunday, during announcements, Sam thanked me, for himself and family. He told the Congregation we had a great trip together - he thought I should get my act together and decide if I was a farmer or carpenter.

"But don't worry Tom, I won't tell what happened to you on the trail ride!"

A STRANGER FOR CHRISTMAS

When you have seen as many Christmases as I you try to remember the best ones. Fortunately, every one was great, always shared with family and friends, with lots of gifts and special food. Of course, the memories of events leading up to the special day will never be forgotten either.

Christmas is always a little more special when you have young children to share it with. Therefore, I go back about twenty some years, when our three girls were preschoolers. Mary always did most of the shopping and decorating, and yes, the cooking too. What did I do, - well, let me see, I always found the perfect tree; those were the days when everyone cut their own natural tree. That was no easy task, as I had more trees rejected than approved. And I always took the three little ones shopping for a gift for their mother.

"That's it," says Mary, as she finishes wrapping the last present and placing it under the tree. "Have you done yours yet?" she asks. "No, I promised the kids I will take them on Saturday." I always wail till the last Saturday, everyone you meet seems to have the real Christmas spirit by then, shaking hands and treating candy, and wishing Merry Christmas.

"Just will not be the same this year though, since Mother moved over to Emily's in Fredericton," I said. She always shared Christmas with us since Father died. "Yes, the kids will certainly miss her," says Mary. "You know, there are lots of lonely people out there who will be spending Christmas alone in their room,-I mean seniors." "You mean down at the home where you work?" I asked. "No, most of them have relatives and friends visit them at Christmas time. I was thinking about Walter Grey who lives at the hotel. He told me it is just like any other day for him. I guess he doesn't have any close relatives in the area."

"Is that the old bachelor that you told me about, he goes

down to your day-care sometimes?" "Yes, he comes twice a week and he found out that we have horses so he is always asking about your team. I guess he was a teamster all his life. Quite a man to drink in his younger years, I understand."

He must be one of those old bums I see shuffling around the town or sitting in the park. I wonder which one he is, I don't know if I care to share Christmas with one of them, I thought. "Do you think we could?" she asked. "He is a real nice old lad, I could ask him tomorrow."

The next day she asked Walter and he agreed, if I could pick him up in the morning and take him back again. After that we told the kids that an older gentleman was going to share Christmas with us. "Like Gramps?" they asked. "Well, about the same age," Mary replied. "Will he have presents for us?" "Maybe not, but you can buy a little present for him if you like," she said.

So next Saturday the kids and I had two people to shop for, their Mom and Walter. We started at Zellers. After touching everything on both sides of the aisle they just had to look over the Barbies and the Cabbage Patch dolls. Ten minutes later on to the cosmetics counter for a bottle of their very best perfume from yours truly. "But what are we going to get Mom," says one, "and Walter," says another. "Well, I was thinking a charm for her bracelet would be nice," so we end up with a silver horse, a heart shape with love printed on it, and a little silver sign that says Mom. Now for Walter; "Over there, just the thing," I said, pointing to the cheapest of their watches. A silver plated Timex pocket watch for less than ten bucks, from all of us I explained, so the clerk wrapped our purchases with pretty paper.

Christmas Eve we went to the school concert, where our oldest had a little part in a play. She had a set of wings attached and had to say "Merry Christmas." We were all pleased with her achievement. That evening they were more excited about meeting

Walter than the arrival of Santa Claus.

Next morning I had to rush down for Walter as Mary prepared breakfast for everyone. As I drove down I wondered what he would look like, and would he be clean. He was waiting in the lobby with a gift box in his hand. A tall lean man, clean and pretty well dressed. Judging by his hair and weather-beaten face, I guessed him to be in his early seventies. We became pretty well acquainted on the way home. I learned that he was born in Nowlanville and left there when he was fourteen to work in the lumber camps. He drove horses most of his life and even knew my father; "drove horses at one of his lumber camps for a few years," he said.

When we arrived at home his eyes surveyed the barns and I knew he was more anxious to see the horses than anything. He presented Mary with his box of chocolates, all wrapped up pretty. She asked if he wrapped it and he explained that the girl at the drugstore wrapped it for him. "She wanted to know if it was for my girl friend," he said with a laugh, "I told her yes, my very best girl friend."

After breakfast we all moved into the living room, and watched as the kids tore into one present after another. Finally they handed Walter his gift, with shaking hand he untied the ribbon and carefully opened the paper to find the pocket watch. His eyes watered a bit as he thanked the kids for their thoughtfulness. He couldn't remember how long it had been since he received a Christmas present.

Since it was a nice day I suggested we should all take Walter back to our sleigh ride camp. Everyone was in agreement, and Walter and I went to the barn to harness up.

"Good looking horses," he remarked, as he steps up beside Dolly the Belgian mare. "How heavy is she?" he asks. "Tell me," I replied. "When I bought her I was told she weighed sixteen hundred. She may have put on a little weight since then." He looked her up and down, and then he said, "sixteen-fifty." "Yes, I would say

116

so, now tell me her age." He looked her over again, felt her withers, looked at her face and then lifted up the upper lip to see her teeth. "She is only a young horse," he replied, "six or seven, no more." "Right again," I replied.

Next he stepped over to look over the gelding, Bruce. Bruce the moose, we often called him, because he had such long legs and was kind of raw-boned. He was probably a cross between a Clydesdale and a Belgian, judging by his hairy feet and the blaze on his face. "This lad is a real power house, I bet; good legs and feet, he must be good in snow." "Yes," I replied, "but he is a little frisky. I have a hard time to hold him back." "Ah- just feeling good, I would like to have him yarding logs for a week or two. What size collar does he wear?" "Twenty-three" I replied, as I passed him the curry comb and brush. "How are you boy?" he asks the horse, as he strokes him with the brush.

I threw the harness over their backs and Walter helped me buckle up. We hooked them up to the bob-sled and picked up Mary and the kids, they had a light lunch with them for the camp. Walter sat up front with me and studied their every step. After a while he says, "Can you tighten up his britchen strap a little, I notice it slipping against his hips; that will chafe him in time." So I tighten it up a little and continue.

"See what I mean," I say to Walter, "he always wants to be ahead of Dolly, I have to keep a tight rein on him all the time." "Try lengthening your traces a link or two on him," he says, "that should help." They step more even after I take his advice. "Here, take the reins," I said as I pass them to him, I knew he was dying to drive. He sat up so straight and proud as he held the reins to that powerful team, I could tell he was happier there then he would be behind the wheel of a new Cadillac.

We arrived at the camp, tied up the horses and rugged them, then we went in and lit a fire in the old cast iron stove. Walter went

117

back out again to be with the horses while Mary and I got the tea and lunch ready. At lunch Walter told us this brought back a lot of old memories, as he spent many a Christmas in the lumber camps.

Someone always had to stay to look after the horses, and since he wasn't married or had any home to go to he would volunteer. "Kept me out of trouble; I would rather be in the woods than hanging around town any day. I used to have a little drinking problem when I was younger," he stated.

Mary had a camera with her and got some good pictures of Walter and the family at the camp, and Walter driving the team. I drove most of the way home as I noticed he was pretty tired. At home again we sat down to our traditional turkey supper. Walter thanked us for having him up and said he had a wonderful day. I drove him back to the hotel and we talked horse most of the way.

Walter continued to go to Mary's day-care at the seniors home, and was overjoyed to receive a few photos of himself and the horses. He showed them to all his friends and kept them propped up on his bureau in his little room. A few months later Mary told me she had some sad news. Walter wasn't feeling good and a check-up found that he had cancer of the liver; the doctor gave him three or four months to live. About three months later Walter died.

We were saddened by his passing, and I always thought of him when I took out the horses, the helpful hints that he gave me. I could have learned a lot from him. The man who at first I thought was a drunken old bum. He was probably a good man, but was caught up by circumstances which he couldn't change.

A few days after his funeral the desk clerk at the hotel called me to stop in sometime I was in town as he had something for me. I picked up the package and opened it when I got home. There was a card with a picture of a horse on it. Inside he had written, "Thank you and your family for making an old man happy, take good care of those horses. Your friend, Walter" Oh yes, there was a shiny pocket watch with a shoe lace attached also.

SMELT FRY

Last Saturday we went down to Flo's Restaurant for the smelt fry. She has two or three fry's every winter. They are very good, pan fried or deep fried. Other restaurants along the Miramichi take alternate Saturdays. We smelt lovers attend as many as possible. You are encouraged to eat hearty, because the price includes, "all you can eat." I generally settle for a plate and a half. Although a few fish lovers sometimes eat three plates; that is all right by the restaurant because with that many smelts one would drink two or three beers.

We used to cook smelts at home, but my wife didn't like the smell left in the house afterwards. The smell was not offensive to me and I tried to encourage her to cook them more often. Every winter there are fish peddlers set up in town, and I often would bring a bag of fresh frozen smelts only to have them stored in our deep freeze.

A few years ago we had a young boarder here from P.E.I. He was one of my daughter's neighbours from Pownell. He didn't know anyone over here so she asked us to take him in for a few weeks as he was taking a refresher course on heavy equipment in Chatham. He turned out to be a real nice chap. I thought I had an ally. I tried a little psychology on the wife at suppertime. I asked Don if he ever tried Miramichi smelts. He replied that he hadn't, he wasn't much of a fish eater. I proceeded to tell him how good they were, especially the winter smelt that is caught out in the bay and frozen right on the ice. It must be the salt water that makes them so firm and sweet, quite a delicacy, I explained. This didn't impress Don at all. My wife had a good laugh as he told me he thought his cat and I would get along real well. Needless to say the smelts stayed in the deep freeze.

All the regulars were at Flo's the other night, everyone

except Carl. I remarked to my wife that I didn't see my old friend Carl; I hope he is all right. We found a seat up in the balcony as the place was full up on the main floor. After a little while Carl and his wife and another couple arrived, they came up to seat near us. As we waited we had a little small talk about the weather and how good it was to see the smelt season start again. It was just something one needed after all that turkey over the Christmas and New Year's season, we agreed.

While waiting, I couldn't help but notice how little he has changed since I first met him fifty years ago. He was still tall and had that half grin all the time, such a good natured guy. We travelled to Moncton every Sunday night and back home again on Friday night. Carl had a big old four door Chevy and it was always filled up with young people, mostly girls.

The two girls who always sat in front with him worked at Eaton's. At that time Eaton's Department Store was the largest employer in Moncton. Carl was studying for his mechanical licence at the Community College. One of the girls in the back was training for a hair dresser. Another worked at an insurance company and the other worked for Blue Cross. I was taking a clerical course at Success Business College.

The roads weren't very good in the wintertime back then. The snow banks were higher than the cars and sometimes quite icy, but Carl kept it on the road. He would give a little chuckle as he straightened her up after slewing sideways and the girls giving a little yelp. I never knew where we were till we stopped. The back windows were always steamed or frosted up. Every now and then there would be a frost heave and one would lean to duck your head as the car lifted up. Packed in the back seat like we were we shifted position quite often. I could see the girls in the front trying to see what was going on in the back as I would give the back of their seat a poke with my foot every now and then.

Well, here comes the girl with two plates with steaming

hot smelts; enough of the daydreams about our road trips. I will enjoy them and probably think of Moncton the next time we meet at a
smelt fry.

SURPRISE BREAKFAST

I have this pesky agent "Roger" in New York, who keeps calling me wanting to know "how's the script coming along?" He keeps reminding me that I only have two months left. He promised the publisher the "new one" would be ready for June. I lied when I said "pretty good" so naturally he wanted me to send him a draft right away. To tell the truth the story was stuck. I had the opening and ending all worked out but the plot still needed some work. I had a bad case of writer's block.

Roger is not a bad guy; he was the first agent to accept my manuscript on Jack's Fate. I had a lot of rejections before he picked it up. He worked with me and suggested a few changes here and there and I went along with him. Then he took it to his publisher and set up promotional stints to promote it to a best seller after several years. By the time that happened, I had another script ready called "Nobody's Fault." He did the same thing with that, it was much easier the second time. I have enough royalties coming in now to keep me going, but I am too young to retire completely.

As you know we are considered "arts people" the same as artists, musicians and sculptors. We act irresponsibly at times and have our peculiar ways. We patronize each other as we are in a class of our own, kind of a free spirit by times. I can go to places all over the world and have affairs with beautiful women. Sometimes I am an Olympic athlete or a wealthy business man. The best of it all is I don't have to leave my chair. So why am I having trouble with this script? Perhaps I should scrap it and start over again. It has become a real challenge, I have put so much time into it that I hate to discard it completely.

I met Keith and his wife at the grocery store as Mary and I were picking up a few things. "How's the new book coming along?" he asked. I told him it was a real struggle and he suggested maybe I needed a change of scenery. "Why don't you go to our cottage, it would be nice and quiet." We all agreed that might work, so I took his keys and bought a few extra groceries for the cottage.

Now ever since I had that little altercation with the law last year my wife has been driving me. "Suspended license," they call it, but it wasn't my fault. One too many beers; I tried to explain to the officer when you're a successful writer you're expected to celebrate now and then. He didn't read books and didn't care who I was, so I still have a few months to go to get my driver's license back.

Mary dropped me off on a Wednesday morning and I told her not to return until noon Saturday. She would have liked to stay a while and started puttering around the camp, shelving the groceries and poking at the fire. I spread my first draft on the table and sat down with my writing tablet. "I needed complete solitude if I am ever going to fix this mess," I told her, as I kissed her goodbye.

I didn't pay any attention to time; I ate whenever I got hungry and slept when I needed to. I nurtured my thoughts with a glass of wine, which I kept on the table with me at all times. It was surprising how well the plot was coming along. It was about a business partnership where one partner and a trusted secretary were trying to manipulate the business so the other partner would give up. Whenever they got the chance they were making deals under the table and depositing the money in a secret account.

By the end of the week I had satisfied my self that I had done a good job. The good guy had persevered after having been tipped off by a part-time helper. The helper was a summer student who was studying business administration but was seen as no threat to the plotting home manager and his evil secretary. In the end everyone received their just reward and the budding student was rewarded with a marriage proposal. Now all I had to do was re-read the whole script, check for misspelling, comas and periods; just little things like that.

My good friend, Keith, is a school teacher at the Big Bear Indian Reservation. There was no school on Friday; it was teacher's conference day. The teachers attended a lecture at the Rodd Hotel and had a lovely buffet lunch. Keith sat with a couple teachers and shared some wine with them as they ate. During the course of the conversation he happened to mention my name and that I was a good friend of his. "In fact he is staying in my cabin upriver," he mentioned. Since they had all afternoon free they thought it would be nice to visit me. The girls liked the idea of meeting a famous writer although they never heard of me before.

Later that afternoon Keith stepped in with a couple of dark-skinned ladies and a couple bottles of Alpenweiss white wine. It was quite a surprise, but a welcome sight since I had been alone for three days. He told me they had the afternoon off and introduced them. They were, tall and slender, taller than either Keith or I, and they had straight black hair half way down their backs. They were both in their thirties. Noni was a couple of years older than her cousin Lena. They were happy to meet me and I let them read a few pages of my manuscript.

The ladies volunteered to wash the dishes that were stacked up on the counter and were overflowed to none end of the table. Keith and I set up the table for a game of cards as Keith popped a wine cork. The rest of the afternoon passed quickly. The game became noisier and more reckless bidding, as the girls beat the boys. In spite of our accusations of their cheating everyone enjoyed themselves.

Around six o'clock, I was starting to get a little hungry. I asked if they would like to stay for supper. To my surprise they decided they would. Keith told us he phoned his wife that he may be late as he was going to visit me. The girls replied they were in no hurry to go back to their apartment, they had nothing pressing to do, only laundry and to prepare for next week's school assignments. We all helped set the table, make a salad and cook up some tomatoes and hamburger. I happened to mention that one could throw spaghetti against the wall and if it was cooked properly it would stick. This started a little spaghetti fight as Nona hit Keith on the neck with her first throw.

We had a great meal and after the mess was cleared up we continued with the cards and the wine. The game became a little more exciting after a while as someone suggested strip poker. We had a great fire on the fireplace and no one minded taking off a few pieces of extra clothing. By the end of the day Keith and I were down to our undershorts and since it was late I decided to call the game off.

Now since everyone had been drinking wine all day we decided it would be beneficial to have a little sleep before getting behind the wheel. There were only two beds. I suggested that I didn't like the idea of sleeping with Keith, that is how stories get started, you know. Noni said that she would lie down with me if I put on all my clothes first, that we could just lie on top of the bedspread. Keith went one further, he said he didn't like sleeping with his pants on. Since it was his camp he felt he had the right to do what he wanted. Surprisingly enough Lena took off her clothes jumped in behind him with only her under-garments on. We turned off the lights and watched the wood crackle and flare for a while. I was soon fast asleep; too much wine always does that to me.

The next morning when I awoke, Noni was beginning to stir behind me. Keith and Lena were still asleep under the blanket. I turned and asked her how she slept. She said she never stirred all night, she had a great sleep. She was a little dry she admitted, and asked me what time it was. I replied that it was eight forty-five; we slept in late as it was so late before we settled in. There wasn't much time left for small talk as the door burst open and in walked our two wives, Jane holding a cardboard tray with four cups of Tim Hortons which fell on the floor.

I'll never forget the expressions on their faces. If I could paint expressions like that I would paint surprise on the faces of our wives and fear on the happy campers. Surprise turned to fury as Jane addressed her husband and the slut in bed with him. Mary didn't say much, she just started cry. She wouldn't give me a chance to explain. The door slammed shut with a loud vibration as they left in a huff. There goes my drive home, I thought.

Everything went downhill after that; the girls were scared and angry at us. They demanded to be taken home immediately. The surprise breakfast was a surprise all right. Keith left with the girls, but, I decided to stay behind. He said he would be back if his wife doesn't let him in, he would like if she would let him get some clothes if nothing else. I knew from a past experience that Mary would take a long time to heal. I might as well stay here. I'll likely have enough time to write another book and I already have a title in mind. How about if I call it "An Innocent Man." If you want to get a hold of me I can be reached at W.W. Bigbear camp. Keith will be sharing the camp with me for a few days I expect.

2020

This is the age of computers, I do not like it or understand it. Computers are running the whole show now, they dictate to people and people worship them like a god. Computers are introduced to children at a very young age, and soon gain more respect than their parents. Every modern home has a computer room, and the whole family take turns in it.

Most of the teaching is by computer. Children start as young as three years old, cartoon characters teach them, ending up each day with a quiz requiring the kid to think. The whole education system for grade school and even college is done through computers at home. However, the children are required to get together a certain number of days to learn social skills. This could consist of public speaking, sports, dancing, home economics, and some volunteer time cleaning public buildings and grounds; this teaches respect for their province.

Industry doesn't employ near as many people as in the past. Much of the work is done by robot and computers. Employees are paid according to their computer skills and social skills. Many people are doing piece work at home; they make one part of a part. The parent company gathers all the parts and assembles them.

We are more diversified than in the past, as only a few years ago we depended entirely on our natural resources. Now we are boasting a car manufacturer, and a small aeroplane factory. We are now making a lot of things out of plastics and steel.

There are boats in the harbour loading and unloading. Tourist ships visit the harbour every other week. The river is promoted all over the world as the home of the salmon. All is being done to encourage tourists to visit as the river is being cleaned up of pollution.

Sport fishing on the river is great as everyone is required to release any fish they catch. The salmon are plentiful and attract fishermen from all over the world. The native Indians have been persuaded that the salmon are contaminated with PCB's so they don't take them for food anymore. Most are employed as river guides.

In spite of all the stress from manufacturing and computing, all the working people are staying fit. It is government policy that anyone on the payroll be required to spend 4 hours each week to keep fit by exercising, and that they spend 4 hours each week doing volunteer work. The employer is required to enforce these activities. The employer also pays them for a 40 hour week, although 32 hours are all that are spent on the job. The employer's are happy with this arrangement as the government has banned unions, and they are getting top production, for a lower rate than before.

Rural areas are less populated and urban areas have expanded. It is government policy to consolidate everything. There are no new building permits allowed for rural people and as soon as the homeowner dies or leaves his home it is taken out or flattened. The government claims that this is best for the people, and they will soon agree, as all the services are easier to administer.

This is also to the advantage of the large corporations as they piece together large blocks of land that used to be settlements.

Those that have good jobs own their own homes in town; enjoy all the good things of life. Those that don't have jobs work for the Province and live in provincial homes. They are required to work at various labour jobs such as thinning the forest and clearing along the roads and rivers. They are supplied everything they need, clothes and food and are bussed to and from work.

Those who have their own low paying jobs live in low rental homes or apartments and generally travel to work by bus. These labourers seldom improve their lot, but they never complain because they know that they are still better off independently than the next step lower, the welfare people, or provincial workers as they are called.

The government has adopted the best of the Capitalist system and the best of the Socialist system to their advantage. The government and Capitalists are pretty well one and the same. Politics are always to the benefit of the wealthy.

A stranger passing through the Province could not help but give a good report. They see beautiful country, sparsely populated, but large prosperous farms. The forests all look like parks, with the trees all evenly spaced, lush and green. The rivers are clear and clean; lots of good fishing. Practically every species of fish is being raised in captivity, and the fish plants are exporting all kinds of fish.

The government boasts of zero unemployment in the Province. It has taken over the Unemployment Insurance, Canada pension and Old Age pensions, and provided housing instead. Anyone who doesn't like the system is free to leave. There is no free lunch here, if your luck gets down you have no alternative but to take up residence with the rest of the paupers at the provincial homes. Once reduced to the provincial workers level one seldom emerges to independence again.

Only the wealthy enjoy the luxury of real food. Everyone else is eating, "bag food," as we call it. The feed companies who used to supply animal feed are now supplying all the government institutions with balanced feed rations. The food is nutritious, doesn't taste too bad, and is easy to prepare, just add an equal amount of water and heat. Just as they used to have rations for chicken growers, laying mash, or dairy rations, so now they also produce young food, middle food and senior food for humans.

Even though the majority of the population is unhappy about the loss of their independence, there is no fear of an uprising. The people in power made sure of that with their planning of such a regime. They introduced the gun law, under the guise that it would be better for everyone's safety. Now very few people own guns and the authorities know who they are.

The plight of the senior citizen is an unhappy one, since the government has taken over all government pensions, whether old age or civil servant. If one hasn't laid away a bundle; or has a good private pension they will surely end up in a provincial senior home. There are a few private senior's homes for the wealthy, but the vast amount of seniors end up here. The end is often quite soon after being assessed, if the panel of social workers deems them useless, they are euthanized as this is widely practiced now, and is considered a compassionate mercy.

The only bright light in the future is the possibility of an Indian takeover, as they are laying claim to all of New Brunswick east of the Restigouche. They have a two hundred year old claim signed by the King of England and they are presenting their claim to the United Nations for assistance. If this fails they claim they will call in warriors from all over North America and physically take over the land. Whites that assist with the takeover will be given reservations to live on; the rest will have to move out.

TED AND ROY

It amazes me, after all these years, that Ted Williams' name is mentioned at nearly every national baseball game. He retired in 1960 with a home run after playing for twenty-seven years for the Boston Red Sox. He still holds the record as the greatest home run hitter ever. Not only was he a great baseball player he was an ace pilot in the Second World War and the Korean War. Some say he liked to fish better than play baseball.

In fact he was a common sight on the Miramichi River. He was known as one of the first conservationists as he seldom kept a fish he hooked. The New Brunswick tourism brochures all showed pictures of the world famous Ted Williams baseball player fishing on the Miramichi. Wherever he went he had his loyal guide, Roy Curtis, by his side. Roy would patiently sit on the shore and often start a little camp fire to heat up the frying pan and boil a cup of tea while Ted tried different flies to raise a salmon.

My memory drifts back to the time I was a small time contractor with a couple of trucks and tractors. Travis Brothers Construction contracted me to dig a basement for them up at the Grey Rapids. I was soon to learn that this fishing camp was being custom built for the famous Ted Williams. It was out in a beautiful field overlooking a stretch of river that had a great salmon pool. Of course this was private water and only the land owner or guests were allowed to fish there.

After digging the basement Harold Travis ordered me to build a driveway to the site also. I was a bit surprised to find out that they were building the camp for New Brunswick tourism. This camp would cost a pretty penny, why would Tourism make a gift to a millionaire, I questioned. Harold explained that it was good public relations and that they would gain a lot more sport fishermen because of his choice to fish here. A couple of weeks later I returned to backfill around the camp which was now partially finished with a lovely verandah overlooking the river.

Hanging on a spike under the verandah was a pair of bib-type chest waders. These were the tallest waders I had ever seen and since I had never met Ted I presumed he must be awful tall. I finished my contract and Travis Construction contacted me that they had a cheque for me. I got another surprise when I received the cheque; it was from the New Brunswick Power Corporation. So, that is how the government works, I thought. If they don't want the people to know how they squander our money they do it through a government corporation like the New Brunswick Power. They have their own way of laundering money. I made my bill out to Travis Construction, they billed tourism and then it goes to N.B. Power. The taxpayers never find out that they made lavish gifts to celebrities such as a camp fully furnished along with electric heat.

Ted hired a local man to act as caretaker, cook and guide. He had a new Ford half-ton with the name of the camp printed on the door. They made quite an impression on the local population as a Mutt and Jeff team; this short stout chauffeur and tall handsome man in the passenger seat. The caretaker was a re-habilitated alcoholic who was a great story teller as well as a camp cook. Some time later I saw the caretaker making his way into town with a battered up truck with no windshield at all. Apparently he "fell off the wagon," and got into Ted's private stock at the camp. Realizing that Ted would be soon arriving he was taking the truck to the dealer to see if he could get a windshield put in.

Shortly after returning Ted replaced both the truck and the caretaker. This time, he hired a teetotaler, Roy Curtis, who became a great friend and accompanied Ted wherever he went. I was surprised to see the two together at Ron's Barber Shop. They were there when I went in and took a seat beside Roy as Ton was giving Ted his brush cut. Ron's was a great place to catch up on the local gossip and he always had a few new jokes as well. The phone rang and Ron answered and had a great conversation, just small talk I presumed. I thought this was strange as he had a celebrity in the chair. He finally finished the cut and Ted stood up, bent over and ran his hand back and forth over the cut brushing out any loose clippings. Straightening up, he twists one way then another, looking in the mirror. He finally nodded his approval and Toy steps up and pays the price as they leave together. When I took my place in the chair I questioned Ron about his treatment to the great Ted Williams. "To tell the truth, Paul, I wouldn't care if he never comes back." Unlike the Dept. of Tourism who went to great expense to claim him, Ron couldn't care less. Ron explained that he was a very fussy man to cut, always telling him how he wanted it to be perfectly flat and checking and moving around as he would be doing his job. To top it all off he never gave a tip, like the rest of his customers. That is why he always lets Roy do the paying. I noticed that and thought it kind of peculiar myself.

We all have some good and not so good points, I suppose. I often noticed where Ted Williams would support fund raisers for various charities along the river. He was also very good about attending as a guest speaker in support of local baseball events. For years he and Roy were a common sight at fishing pools and the community of Miramichi. He made many friend s and loved to talk fishing and supported the conservation of salmon and the local salmon hatchery.

He was very instrumental in the banning of set nets in the tidal waters. It was his theory that they were taking an unfair amount of breeding stock out of the river. Roy Saunders ran the local service station; he also had a license and fished a set net. Ted always stopped in to gas up as he passed by. He and Mr.

Saunders would always get into an argument over the decline of salmon in the river.

It was great sport for the local boys who congregated around the pop cooler smoking and getting the local news. Ted blamed the set nets, Saunders blamed the sport fishermen, who were allowed to fish long after the set nets were required to be taken up. It looked like Roy was losing the argument as Ted claimed that he and most sport fishermen released the fish, to go on up the river to spawn after they carefully removed the hook. Finally Roy says the fish are too far spent, after being played up and down the river for a half hour that they don't recover. They go away and die and float down the river in a few days.

Williams said he couldn't see any sport in catching fish and clubbing them to death such as Saunders and a dozen or so others, who set nets, did. They were destroying the fishery. "At least we kill our fish instantly in a humane way with one blow to the head. Not like you sport fishermen, who torture them to death." Ah there is no sense arguing with you," Ted replies as he turns to leave. "Just a minute" Roy says, following him out to the paved parking lot. "Suppose you lend me your rod, I could put a piece of meat on a hook and catch a cat. Then I could let her run over there and reel her in a few times. How long do you think it would be before someone landed to take me away?" Ted sputtered, that Roy didn't know what he was talking about and it wasn't the same thing.

The boys around the cooler had a great laugh as Roy stepped back in the garage. You sure told him Roy, they agreed.

Well they still remained great friends. Ted still stopped in for gas and a little argument. Years later the Dept. of Fisheries noticed what Ted had been saying all along that the salmon were declining each year in alarming numbers. More conservation had to be practiced or the salmon stock would be eliminated.

As a result the Federal Government bought back the set

net licenses from the few fishermen who still fished. Another major deterrent that helped clear the river was a fine of one thousand dollars for the first time poachers and jail time for repeat offenders. The fishing patrol was stepped up and motion cameras were set up everywhere. Along with a cutback on the high seas, especially up around Iceland, where the salmon made their migration to feed on the shrimp grounds.

Well, Ted and Saunders have both passed away now. I bet if they should meet in the hereafter they will still argue who was right about the salmon fishing.

THE ONE CENT PIECE

I picked up a few things and stepped up to the counter of the convenience store. A couple teen aged boys were impatiently waiting their turn in line behind me. In my haste to pick up my parcels and pocket the change at the same time I dropped a coin. It could be a nickel or dime. When I stepped back to see what it was I discovered it was only a penny. I picked it up without giving it a thought.

The next in line stepped around me in disgust while his friend made a remark "Don't throw your money away old timer." I could tell it was meant in jest so I ignored him and made my exit. As I got into my car I wondered if I should have left it lying on the floor. "One for the sweeper" I could have replied and walked away looking cool.

However, I am from the old school, "look after the pennies and the dollars will look after themselves." I remember when I was a happy young lad with a couple of cents in my pocket looking at the candy counter trying to decide the best value. Then there was the big piggy bank on my dresser. That taught me to save my pennies for dollars. We would unload it at Christmas time, roll the pennies and receive enough for a few presents.

The cent has lost a lot of respect over the years. One shop keeper tells me he often sees young lads toss their pennies out of their change into the parking lot. You always get a few cent coins back when you make a purchase. However, you very seldom see anyone count out the exact change when making a purchase, even though they could do it easily if they had the time.

Every now and then I have to unload some change into a coffee cup on my dresser. There is generally some charity collecting coins that will be glad to receive the unwrapped change. Enough pennies gathered together can buy a wheelchair for a needy child. On a happier occasion they could help send a needy child to a summer camp.

If you take a close look at a cent coin you might be surprised at the clarity of the print and picture. As everyone knows the Queen's head is on one side and the Maple Leaf on the other. Heads or tails as we know it. The head is of the Queen Elizabeth the second. She celebrated fifty years of reign in two thousand and two and is still ruler of the British Empire we can rest assured that any aggressor country would have to deal with the whole British armed forces.

The other side of the coin, "the tail side" has a few Maple leafs engraved on it. This is our national symbol; it reminds us this is a Canadian coin. It is the official currency for all of Canada including Quebec. The leaves are different in size by joined at the stem the same as the sizes of the provinces differ, but all together produce a great country.

Some one cent pieces have been around nearly as long as I. It is surprising they show little wear over the years. How many hundreds of miles have they travelled. Always under cover, in a pocket with other change, or in the bottom of a lady's purse with a large assortment of other things. It has been held by a sweaty hand of a youngster in fear of losing it. It has been pinched by some old spinster as she places it in her little change purse. Passed from one hand to another both clean hands and dirty ones, its copper finish allows it to withstand all the abuse over the years.

As I look at the change in my hand I notice a couple of new looking one cent pieces in amongst the dull ones. The older ones have a dull light brown finish but the picture and lettering are still in good shape and all show the date they were minted. These two new looking ones are six and two years old. They have a pinkish orange colour, or one might call it rose. They are beautiful if looked at as jewelry.

Now that is an idea I could use. I could drill a little hole in them and run my wife's gold hoop earrings through them. That would add some flash to those earrings, and when she wears them I could remind her she is worth two cents more. On second thought it might be better to keep the cents in my pocket.

THE AMERICAN

We heard a car in our driveway; it was a big car with a foreign license plate. The car was slowly shuttling back and forth. The driver was obviously lost or else scared of our big old yellow dog that was waiting to greet the stranger. Finally he turned the car off and got out to pat old "Jake" on the head.

"Who could that be?" Mary asked. "Go out and see what he wants, before that dog gets his muddy paws on him."

"Well, give me a chance to get my boots on. I don't like running out to meet everyone that comes in the yard like a bootlegger or something."

The gentleman met me half-way still patting Jake, who already made a new friend. "Nice dog," he says, "hi, my name is John Cavenaugh." Now that is a name I haven't heard for awhile I thought.

"Tom Bryenton," I offered my hand.

"Well Tom, I am on a kind of a wild goose chase," offers the tall greyish aged gentleman, with a broad smile.

"Well John," I replied, "Cavenaugh isn't it? Now that is not a common name around here, although it used to be one time, I guess. What can I do to help you?'

"You have heard of the Cavenaughs then?" he asked.

"Oh yes, my old neighbour, Mr. Parks, often spoke of the Cavenaughs who used to live out by the river. But there hasn't been any Cavenaughs around here for years."

"Well that is why I am here, you see I am getting old and I am trying to find my roots. I would like to pass on what history I can dig up to my grandchildren. My grandfather Isaac used to live somewhere around here, I understand."

"I think I could show you the place. Bill Parks showed me an old stone basement on the next property down from mine here.

Would you like to see it, I am not too busy today?"

"I, I don't want to impose on your kindness," he stammered.

"Not at all, I'll just tell Mary where I'm going. I'll grab some bug spray; there may be a few flies out there today."

Mary insisted that we should have a glass of cool lemonade before going out there.

Over a tall glass at the picnic table Tom, and Mary, who had joined them, learned a lot about the stranger.

"You see," he began, "my father Charles left the Miramichi when he was a very young man. He was Isaac's only son but he had two sisters who also moved away later. His intention was to go work in the lumber woods down in Minnesota. He thought he could help his poor old dad by sending some money home; which he did, till the old folks died. Bye and bye he met a lady from Massachusetts and they got married.

They settled in Pittsburg and Dad went to work in an iron foundry. He did well and raised in his rank, soon he was a supervisor. The owner took a liking to him and offered to sell him the business. He could pay for it over a number of years. The owner was getting old and just wanted out.

Dad just got started when World War I broke out. He did a thriving business for the U.S. Army. He made everything from steel helmets to ammunition jackets for the big guns. Help was scarce but everyone did their part. He even employed a lot of women, they were great workers.

The factory continued to expand, and he survived the depression. At that time he was making railroad rails and wheels. I joined the family business about that time and I sold the business about twenty years ago. The unions were so strong they were practically running the business. Then the environmentalists started giving us a hard time. I got a chance to sell to a larger firm so I got out with a little nest egg. My three children all got a good education and they didn't want any part of it.

After we sold the factory we moved to Massachusetts. We bought a little acreage out by Lake Tahoe and had quite a few good years. I have five grandchildren and they like the country. My wife became sick last year and died during the winter. "Now my children are watching over me like a child," he says with a little chuckle. "I always wanted to visit the Miramichi but could never find the time, you know how it is. Time goes by so quickly, now I just have too much time without Ethel. I told my son I was going up to Canada, he thought I was crazy. Enough about me, have you lived here long, you have a beautiful place."

"Oh yes," we answered in unison, "but we love to travel," Mary kept on. "We have family in P.E.I. and Alberta. We have six grandchildren."

"We had better get going," I interrupted. "See you when we get back, Mary."

"Thanks for the refreshing drink, Mary, hope to see you again," says John, as he heads for my half ton sitting under the big oak tree.

"We can drive right out to the river with this old truck," I told him. "On the back" I ordered Jake who was ready to join in the cab.

"What a beautiful river," John remarked as I parked the truck on our cottage lot. "You have a cottage too?" he remarked as he looked over the log cabin with the verandah extended out over the crest of the river hill.

"Yes, it is small, only two bedrooms. I built it for my family when they all land here on their holidays. They like it a lot and sometimes I rent it out to sport fishermen for a week or two. "Helps recover the cost," I say with a chuckle.

"Is there anyone in it now?" John asks.

"No, not today."

"Well, could you show it to me?" he asks as he makes his way to the door.

"Yes, I'll get the key out of the truck here."

As he stepped up on the verandah he was awe struck with the river view. "Yes, it's pretty nice out here," I agreed as I opened the door. He looked it over very carefully; finally he went over to the wall and rubbed his hand over a log like a blind man might. "Did you build this cabin yourself?" he asked.

"Yes, every bit of it," I proudly exclaimed. It was not every day now that anyone notices anything that I have accomplished.

"And the logs, did you find them as well?"

"Yes, I cut them right here on my own property."

"You certainly did a wonderful job of building it," he remarked, still looking back at it as we started for the next property below. "Is it far?" he asked as we entered the property, all grown up with alders, poplars and white birches.

"No, just follow me, only about five minutes," I suggested. As we meandered in and out between the small trees, John would pause whenever he would get a glimpse of the river below. I tried to imagine what was going through his mind as he trod on the old homestead.

Finally we came to the old basement site. It was merely a depression in the ground with a lot of rock scattered unevenly on the bottom. Wild roses were growing amongst them. Close by there was a huge clump of lilac bushes. The larger ones in the center were twisted and bent in every direction but still they were loaded with blossoms.

Some people might think there wasn't much to see but to John, it was like coming home after a long journey. "So this is where Isaac and Sarah settled, it is so beautiful. I wish Ethel could have seen it." He rested his back against a small tree as he surveyed the site. "The lilacs are lovely; do you suppose they were planted here when my grandparents lived here?"

"Yes I do, every old place along the river has the same thing; Lilac and wild roses and an old apple tree or two. What more does a person need?" I asked with a laugh.

"Yes, we never know when we are well off," he agreed.

"A little piece of ground to grow a garden, a field to keep a horse and a cow, lots of timber for winter fuel. It was a pretty simple life I guess. Oh yes, the river was full of salmon then and there was lots of wild game, deer and moose for the taking. The neighbours were few and far between but they were all neighbourly and helped each other out."

"Good air and water too," John added, as he peered into the pile of rocks. "Not much left of the old house is there."

"No, only a few foundation rocks but enough to mark the site, however." Just then I noticed an old black piece of iron sticking out of the ground. Since I was the only one wearing boots I carefully made my way in to investigate. It was a rounded handle, with a little tug up came an old cast iron teapot. The bottom was missing but the sides and spout was in pretty good shape. I hoped up with the prize and handed it to him.

"Here is Isaac's teapot," I said, "the bottom is missing but it is still in pretty good shape, might make a nice flower pot."

"Oh thank you, Tom, but you found it; perhaps Mary would like to have it."

No, it is yours from your grandfather. It was waiting for you to return."

"Well I am here now, thank you so much, I will cherish it forever."

After that we walked down by the site a little and John noticed the beautiful view he could see down river for three miles. He also noticed a few nice cottages on either side. "People are all trying to get back to the river," I noted. Some pretty nice cottages going up every year."

"I would like to have one like yours," John remarked. "The people that own this property now, do they use it?"

"Not much," I replied "they live out by the highway. Old Dan and his wife are all alone now, and not in very good health either. Awful nice old man though, loves to talk about the old days."

"Do you think he would sell it?" asked the American. "Everything has its price, and I wouldn't mind paying top dollar to have this property. Would you see him and give me a call as I have to return home tomorrow. I wasted too much time in the archives; I should have come here first."

He kind of riled me a bit when he started talking about money and "everything has its price." Just like all Americans, I thought, he just doesn't know any better. Just then a thought hit me, there might be a little bit in this deal if I work it right. After all he has lots of money and I could always use some.

"I'll see him and let you know," I promised. When we returned to my house it was lunch time. Mary insisted that John should dine with us as we didn't have company. That along with the smell of fresh biscuits coming out of the kitchen made it impossible to refuse.

John enjoyed the home cooked meal and told us more about his family. Before he left he enquired if he could rent our cabin for a week in October. He was sure some of his family members will come with him. "I may have to pay them to come," he chuckled. "Once they see this place they won't want to leave, I am sure of it."

As he left he shook hands with us again and said he has a special place for the old kettle on his mantle back home. He was no sooner out of the yard when I went out to see my old neighbour, Dan Carruthers. I told him about my visitor and asked if he would like to sell. He said he would consider it if the price was right. He is not much different than the American, I thought, except the American has the money and we don't.

He didn't think he wanted to sell the house but if a good offer came along for the front field, he called it, he would consider it as he wasn't using it. The front field contained thirty-five acres and hadn't been a field for the last forty years as there were large trees growing up in it now.

"You know, I was offered twenty thousand for it a few years ago. How much do you think its worth?" he asked me.

"That is up to you to say as it is your land."

"Do you think I should double the offer, say forty thousand?" he asked while wringing his hands, "I don't want to scare him off."

"I don't think that will surprise him. Forty thousand Canadian is not so much to an American. Tell you what; I'll see how much he is willing if you will split the difference for anything over. This deal will just be between me and you, you understand."

"Go for it," says Dan, "see what you can get and we will split anything over forty, when will I know how you make out?"

"In a couple of weeks, no doubt," I suggested.

A couple of weeks later I phoned John and told him I had talked to Dan. He was a little reluctant, I told him, but he finally agreed to sell all the front property except his house, one acre.

"How much does he want?' John interrupted.

"Well, there is thirty-five acres and waterfront property is pretty high. He has turned down some pretty good offers, he told me. You know, there are at least three cottage lots out there."

"How much?" John asked again.

"He said he wouldn't take anything less than eighty thousand."

"Take it," says John. "Thanks, my friend, and I'll send the

money when the deed is ready."

When I hung up the phone I told Mary I just made twenty thousand and there may be more. He will be wanting someone to do the building for him and he will need a caretaker, nice job for an old lad," I laughed.

"Yes, that is great, now we will be able to go out West again, and if you land that job we will be able to go south this winter.

So much for the twenty thousand, I thought. Oh well, easy come easy go.

THE GREAT TREE

Every morning as I sat at the kitchen table I would scan
the horizon to see the great tree. As sure as I sprinkled a spoonful
of brown sugar on my oatmeal, I would look back to see if it was
still standing. We went back to see it one time, my dad on
snowshoes and my brother David and I on the March crust. That
was a great day. We finally got to see the giant up close. We tried
to join hands as we spanned the tree with our arms. As we gazed
up the tall tree we wondered what the view would be like from
the top. One could probably see Crocker Lake and the Miramichi
River from the lookout at the top. However, there were no limbs
near the ground; one would need a tall ladder to reach the bottom
limbs.

Father explained to us that it was a white spruce. He was a
lumberman and did a good bit of travelling in the woods as he
laid out winter cutting sites for lumber camps. He told us that it
was unusually large for its species. White pine and hemlock are
often that large, but not spruce. Perhaps it was so healthy because
it lived close to the spring and it had a good source of water at all
times. As we drank from the spring ourselves we had to agree
with him, the water was so clear and cold. A straight line of
blazed trees marked the boundary. The tree was only one hundred
feet from the westerly line.

Was it the size or the memory of that wonderful day that
caused me to have such admiration for it? I tend to think of the
latter. Two young boys went for a hike in the woods with their
best friend, their dad, and what a wonderful day we had. Father
was a very busy man; he was in charge of a large lumbering
business. In his spare time he conducted business with clients at
home talking on the telephone. He also supervised a small
farming operation on our home farm. We lived on a one hundred

acre farm that bordered on the Miramichi River and was almost two miles deep. Our farm was about fifty percent cleared land and fifty percent woodlots.

You see, David and I were only two of six children and a wife vying for a little attention from such a busy man. But that day we had him all to ourselves, or so we thought. You see Father always mixed pleasure with business, and this day he had brought his axe with him. As we scattered along on the March crust he would brighten up the spots on the line trees. A property line has to be maintained every now and then in order to keep in good with ones neighbour. It has to be easy to see so no one cuts across the line from either side. Every fifteen or twenty years the blazes get hard to find as some line trees blow down or the blazes heal over. It is a good idea to reblaze and blaze some new trees that are on the line.

That day, after spending a little time at the big tree and spring, we pressed on another half mile to the big yellow birch blazed on all four sides. This was our westerly corner, he explained. Then it was due East seventeen rods across the back line to the Cedar blazed on all four sides. Then we started for home following the property line in a southerly direction. Father blazed trees as we walked along. The crust was beginning to give away and every now and then we would poke a leg through. Father would invite one and then the other of us to climb on the back of his snowshoes and although awkward, it was better than slumping through first one leg than the other. We returned home about mid-afternoon, tired but happy. A tall glass of fresh buttermilk and a large hump of molasses cake was a refreshing break.

By some strange twist of fate I am the one who ends up with the farm. I always had a love for farming as well as lumbering. This little farm provided both, but not enough to make a living so both my wife and I worked away from home. My farming and lumbering operation provided little income but a lot of enjoyment. My wife and three daughters were always happy to be part of it. Our two eldest daughters now live on farms of their own and we visit them frequently. Our youngest, Karla, married Dean and they have one daughter, Jenna. They like farming so well they built a new house out at the river and they tend to their horses and cattle. Dean is a carpenter and he works at his trade by day and on the farm all the other time, and loves it.

When we came back from wintering at our daughter's in Alberta my son-in-law, Dean, was cutting some lumber on the home farm. He pretty well runs the farm now since my wife and I are retired. We kind of like to travel when we feel like it. We had been married to the farm for thirty-five years and, although it was a happy marriage, there was no place for travel in it. Cows and horses have to be tended to daily, to say nothing about the care of the apple orchard. He loves to farm, sort of reminds me of myself when I was younger.

"You know that big tree back there?" he questions.

"Yes, what about it?" I asked as I looked to see it still standing. He knew I didn't want anyone to cut it.

"I would like you to have a look at it; I think it may be dying."

I agreed to go have a look with him although I suspected he was just looking for an excuse to cut it. I had been defending that tree for a long time now. Different people cutting pulp and logs for me wanted to cut it but I always refused.

As we approached the giant tree up close I was surprised to see the limbs at the top were dead. It would only be a short time until rot set in and it would be worthless.

We agreed the tree should be cut, Dean said he wanted some lumber to make some repairs to the barn. There would be some lovely boards in the butt log there to make a new floor for the hay wagon.

How would he handle it, I wanted to know. He had it all worked out, Paul Dunn was cutting the next lot to us. He would yard the logs with his porter and then take them up to the sawmill and saw them out for us. The next morning we set out to fell the tree. I regret I never thought of the camera at the time. Dean cut a big undercut; then proceeded to saw around the trunk. The tree just stood there and teetered back and forth a little. It was still attached in the middle and the cutting bar couldn't reach any further. Our only hope was that the wind would catch it and finish off the job for us. Our plan was to fell it in a bit of an opening from a previous cut. We were at the mercy of the wind and we began to make wedges to drive in the chainsaw cut to tip the tree in our favour. Finally a big wind came up and with a loud crack the tree began to fall, not quite where we had planned as there was a big maple tree in its path. It hit that hardwood and broke it in two like a match stick.

AS we gazed at the fallen giant we agreed we got it just in time as there was some ground rot in the butt of the log. We examined the stump which was forty two inches at the cut. How old was it, we wondered, and then we counted the rings. Some were one half inch apart, those were good growing years. As the rings approached the outside they became closer and closer together, obviously it had been done growing for some time. There were about one hundred and forty rings; that's how old the tree was. I thought it might have survived the great Miramichi fire of eighteen twenty-five, but not so. When we finished cutting up the tree we had three sixteen foot logs, one twelve and two eight foot blocks of pulpwood. There was about ten feet of top left which had broken in the fall. Therefore the tree was over eighty feet tall.

A couple of weeks ago Paul phoned Dean to tell him he would pick up the logs on Saturday. Paul left his truck out by the highway and was in the process of loading the logs when a passing car stopped and a gentleman came into where they were. He said he would like to buy that big log as he was one of the men who ran a post and beam manufacturing plant in the industrial park. Dean told him it wasn't for sale as he had plans for it himself. The man offered him five hundred dollars for it hoping he would change his mind.

After he left Paul asked Dean if he realized that the tree with its three other logs, was worth surely worth one thousand dollars. "Do you have anymore on your lot?" he laughed.

Paul manufactured the log to Dean's specifications and delivered a whole truck load of lumber to the farm. We marveled at all the lumber from one tree, over fifteen hundred board feet. He said he was sorry, but he had to cut two feet of the butt of the big log in order to get it into the mill. I told him that was alright as now I will have a lovely flower pot, all I have to do is cut out the center with the power saw.

I miss the tree when I look back at the woodlot, but I am happy it is still on the farm. The big six by sixes support the barn floor and the three by sixes make the floor. The new wagon platform is all made from it and I have the flower pot for a conversation piece, what do you think?

"There is more." What more can there be you ask.

Well there is a mysterious hole in the ground only about one hundred feet from where the tree grew. It is about eight feet in diameter, a perfect circle and most times it is full of water, but last winter it was dry. There is a lot of muck in the hole and one can surge a small pole down about twelve feet before hitting bottom.

Some people that have seen it suggest that someone, sometime, must have started to dig a well there. But there is no burn around it and why would anyone want to dig a well with a spring only a couple of hundred feet away.

I was telling my geologist friend, Ben, about it and he suggested that it might have been caused by a fallen meteorite. If there is ever an excavator in the area I am going to get him to dig down and see what is in the bottom. Who knows, you might see a meteorite sitting beside the big flower pot on our lawn! Wouldn't I have something to talk about then?

THE HANDY MAN

Joe Jones was a handy man; he lived alone with his dog. One day an old flame calls him to come out to fix her washing machine.

As he rattles along the road Joe tries to remember that day, long ago, that the four of them spent at the lake. It was about twenty years ago, he re-visits the scene every time he gets a glimpse of her whenever their path crosses. Water under the bridge, he mused, he doubts if she even remembered. She still owns the camp, he had heard, her father left it to her. I wonder if they go out there very often.

This must be the house, he thought as he turned in the driveway. Yup, this is the place all right, as Susan opened the door and stands there as he picks up his tool box. She looks as good as ever, no - better, he corrected his thought. She smiled as he walked up to her. How could Howard leave such a beautiful woman to go out to the oil fields? He must have been really hard up.

"Well hello Joe, how are you? You're looking great."

"Hello Susan, I am just fine. I might say you are looking great as usual. Are you having a little trouble with your washing machine?

"Yes, the stupid thing just quit on me," she says as she leads the way to the basement.

"How old is it?" Joe asks trying to keep his mind on business although the long bronze legs in the crispy white shorts were distracting.

"It is not very old," she says, "only a couple of years I think, but then time goes by so quickly, doesn't it?"

"Yes indeed," says Joe, thinking of that day at the lake again.

Joe turns the dials of the washing machine but nothing happens. "Seems like a power problem," he says, "have you checked the breakers?"

"Yes, they all seem O.K. Right over here, have a look."

"I'll pull her out a take a look at the motor," Joe suggests. When he pulls the machine out, he notices the plug-in cord is just about all the way out. "This might be it," he tells her, "only a loose plug-in. It must have vibrated out. I'll just spread the prongs a little so it will stay in."

"Well, I'll be," says Susan, "what could cause that?"

"You know," says Joe, "this is a fairly heavy cord and a washing machine vibrates pretty bad at times, I suppose it just worked out of contact."

"It sure does vibrate by times," Susan agrees. "Sometimes I think I should sit on it, might give me quite a thrill. Especially now since Howard has been away for nearly three months." She grabbed his arm as she bent over laughing. "Might give an old girl quite a thrill," she adds as she sobers up.

"Yes" agreed Joe, "but you would have to be on the same cycle. I don't believe such a beautiful woman should have resort to a washing machine for their kicks," he says with a laugh. "I would hate to be rated second to a washing machine."

She knew him well enough that she didn't hold anything back. She could give it or take it so she said what she was thinking in a joking manner.

"In other words don't try the washing machine, try the washing machine repair man. Something like that song you hear now-a-days, "save a horse, ride a cowboy." But my cowboy is still out West, what is a poor girl supposed to do," she says with a sigh.

Joe shoves the washing machine back in place and picks up his tool box. "That was an easy fix,' he joked.

"Yes, I am happy it wasn't serious. I feel stupid bringing

you out here for something I should have noticed. How much do I owe you?' she asked.

"Not a thing," Joe replies, "it was nice seeing you again."

"You sure; well, how about a drink? I would love to have a drink with you. What would you like?'

"A beer will be just fine," as he sat down at her table.

Between sips of beer they brought each other up to date since they graduated from high school twenty years ago.

Finally she dropped it. "Remember that day down at the lake. I really wanted to be with you but Helen was my best friend then and she always had the hots for you, you know. She was the lucky one I guess, did you know that young James was conceived at the lake that night. Howard was happy when he found out that we would have to get married and I wouldn't be going off to college anyway. Howard is kind of jealous of me, or might I say overprotective. You know he used to phone me at work to make sure I was there. I never thought he would go out West let alone stay so long."

"He must like it," Joe offered, "I hear the money is good."

"Money isn't everything; I know it first hand from working at the bank these last seventeen years. You make out alright and you are a free person. Howard often said he admired your lifestyle.

"Perhaps he would like to trade places for a while," Joe suggested. "Then he could go home to be welcomed by a dog and I a beautiful woman. It is not all it is cracked up to be," he said with a laugh. "Well, I must be on my way," he said, going for his tool box.

"Just a minute," she said, "would you mind having a look at my shower, it has a constant drip and I want to pay you," she insists.

"O.K." says Joe, "let's have a look; it seems like the

shower head is leaking at the inlet. He unscrews it, takes some teflon tape, from his tool box and makes a few wraps on the pipe threads. "That should do it," he says with a smile. He is reaching up replacing the shower head when she squeezes in behind him and presses her body tight to his back while reaching around to put her hand on his bare chest inside his shirt.

"You look so good I just couldn't resist," she says, still holding her arm around him. Then he pulled him down to her and they kissed. "Come on, I am going to pay you," she says leading him into the bedroom and closing the door behind them.

"I have been wanting to do this for about twenty years," she confessed, as they kissed and caressed each other.

"Me too," Joe assured her, "are we safe here?"

"Yes, we are safe till supper time; I won't tell if you don't."

"Well, no one will ever know then" says Joe as he slips in bed beside her.

After that there were little rendezvous at the lake, Joe's place and occasionally the repair man called at her place. Susan was no longer lonely as they had lots of telephone conversations whenever the coast was clear. They were getting a little careless with their new-found love affair and had a few close calls.

No secret is foolproof and some friends began to notice little give-a-ways that something was going on. Someone mentioned to Susan that the repair man seemed to be making a lot of calls to her place. "Is everything breaking down?" they asked. One of Joe's friends chided him at the Legion one night after a few too many drinks. He asked him if he was having a good time with Howard's wife, and he had better be careful when Howard comes home.

A few quick months went by; Joe was both happy and sad. He felt bad about sneaking around with his friend's wife. On the other hand he was happy that he finally got the chance to have an affair with Susan, the girl he often wished to be with for over twenty years. Now he really knew what she was like but just as glad she belonged to someone else.

One night Susan informed him that their good times would have to stop, as she got a call from Howard. He said he was flying down on Friday.

"Does he know anything about us?" Joe whispered.

"I don't know, of course I will deny everything and you too if he should consult you."

"Of course," Joe agreed, swallowing a big lump that came up in his throat, with the thought of Howard coming at him. He knew he would be no match for the man who was known to have a vicious temper.

She wept as he held her, she told him she was sorry Howard was returning and that she liked him better. She had a great summer and was thankful that he rescued her from the washing machine.

Joe asked if they should try to meet occasionally.

"No," she said, "afraid not, you don't know what a jealous man Howard is, it would be too risky. He said he was coming home for the winter and that he might go out again next spring. I'll miss you so much, what are you going to do?"

Joe gave a little cough. "I guess I'll go out West for the winter, I hear there is lots of work for electricians, and maybe I'll see you next summer."

THE RACE HORSE

In the year of nineteen twenty the main transportation routes were the rivers. Of course, all the small rivers ran into larger rivers which ran out to the bay. The town of Milltown was established on the bank of the great Beaver River where the water at the wharf was deep enough to accommodate ocean going vessels. The river system was the main transportation route. Automobiles were beginning to surface in the towns but the roads were poorly constructed and cars didn't perform very well. Railroads were being built to connect with Upper Canada.

Milltown was a busy little town with three saw mills within two miles of river. The wharf was always a busy spot. Schooners would come in with loads of potatoes and salt cod from P.E.I. Some came in with loads of coal from Cape Breton. Other schooners arrived from the West Indies with loads of sugar, molasses and rum. Horses were used to haul supplies to and from the wharf. Lumber was the main export and there was generally a large steamship being loaded for the overseas market.

The ferry wharf was also a busy spot two or three times a day. Horse cart taxis met the river boats which covered a twenty mile radius. These river boats hauled general freight and passengers to and from town.

Most of the people upriver were employed in the lumber camps. Every community had a contractor who would look after "a job," a winters cut of lumber for one of the wealthy lumber barons. A lumber camp generally employed about thirty men and almost as many horses.

Mike Donovan ran a job for Matchett's Lumber Co. He lived on a farm in the little community of Connors. Most of the men from the community worked in the camp for Mike. Some had their own teams and others used Mike's horses. The men went to the camps in the fall and worked six days a week. Many men only got home for a short visit once a month. They used horses and bobsleds to transport the logs to the river. There they were put in large piles called "landings." After the ice ran out in the spring the logs were dumped into the river and floated down to the lumber mills. This was called "the drive."

When Mike settled up with Matchett Lumber Co. after his logs were in he realized he had a good year. He decided he needed a couple more teams of horses for the up-coming season. Teamsters preferred work horses from P.E.I. because they were tame compared to Western horses. They were more used to the harness and easier to shoe. Some Western horses never had harness or shoes on before.

The Donovans were enjoying their good fortune and finally had a little money to spare. Mike told his wife his plan to go to the Island. Joe, who was in his last year in school, asked if he could accompany him. He had never been to the "Garden in the Sea," and would love to go with his Dad. Mike made reservations with a schooner captain that was unloading potatoes at the town wharf. The return trip would take about a week.

On arrival at the wharf at Summerside they soon found out who had some good horses for sale. Some farmers were beginning to use steam tractors for tilling the large fields, and were able to cut back on their horses. Harness racing was the big sport there and since they had some time before returning home they went to see some races. Of course to make the race more exciting one has to place a little wager. Mike was impressed by Joe's good judgment of both horse and driver. When the race was over they were a little ahead of the game.

The next day found them back at the track again. They wanted to go through the stable and look over the fine horses. Everyone was friendly with them and anxious to talk horse. When they found out Mike was over from the mainland buying work horses they suggested he should buy a good race horse. One of their friends fell on some hard luck and had a half dozen to sell. His stable is at the end of Barn Two, he has good horses, it's a pity he has to sell but there was sickness in the family.

"No harm to look," Mike says, as they find the stable." These horses come from the best blood lines on the Island," the trainer told them. The proven racers ranged from fifteen hundred to three thousand but there were also some young horses just being trained, they would be considerably less. He had a two year old filly that he said he would sell cheap, she has good possibilities but it would cost him a lot for training and board. "A bargain at five hundred," he told Mike. Mike said he just paid that for four work horses. He talked it over with Joe who said he would love to have her and that he knew he could train her himself. So, on a sudden impulse they bought the beautiful little racer called Molly.

On their way home Mike told Joe the horse was his but he didn't want anyone to know how much she cost. They decided that they wouldn't race her until she was good and ready. She would have to be well cared for, good food and lots of exercise. Since Joe had eight miles to go to high school he could drive her in a cart back and forth. Every day he would open her up on the good stretches of road. She loved to run and the two enjoyed their outings. After the river froze Joe hooked her up to a sleigh. The time was much faster on ice as the sleigh was smooth and hardly noticeable behind her.

Back in those days there were lots of trotting horses along the river. The highways were not paved and poorly plowed in the wintertime. For a few months every winter the automobile was laid up. The frozen river was the main transportation route and horse and sleigh replaced the car. One could count half dozen horses on the ice at any time. Of course everyone knew who had the fastest horse and envied the position.

Joe knew Molly was fast but he didn't know how fast until he was challenged by the first place horse in the community. 'She took him with ease," he told his father, Mike. Mike advised him not to let it go to his head. In fact he cautioned him not to show his horse's speed too much if he wanted to enter Molly in the big Easter Run-Off in Milltown. If he exercised his horse every day and raced against the clock he could monitor the progress and decide if his horse was ready.

The Easter Run-Off was the biggest winter event of the year for horse fanciers. It took place on the ice just upriver from town. There was a half mile track marked off between two painted poles. It was a straight line and started with a pistol shot whenever the horses were all lined up.

There were a half dozen different classes. One was for horses under three years. There was another for three year olds, which Molly would qualify; another for first timers. Then there were a couple grudge races where only two top contenders wanted to prove whose horse was the fastest for once and all. All these classes would lead to the big "free for all" where anyone who thought they had the fastest horse of all could enter. This was the highlight of the day and many of the horses that ran in an earlier class would be contenders. Naturally there was a lot of betting going on amongst the fans.

There was a lot of excitement leading up to the big day. Town people would prepare at the site for weeks leading up to the race. Two or three horses would compete as they exercised. Curious spectators would be seen out on the ice or watching from a distance as they tried to pick a winner. There was a lot of money to be made betting if one could call the winner. The moneyed people like the doctors, lawyers, and businessmen had the best horses. Very little was known about the country entries as they were of little threat.

If one wanted to get any information on the competition just hang out at the blacksmith shop for a little while. Everyone took their horse to Dave's Blacksmith Shop for a professional fit. Dave made the sharpest shoes; he fitted them like an orthopedic doctor would. Often times a race horse may have had an injury to one of its feet. He would have to fit a special shoe to make the horse more comfortable.

There were always a few older horse lovers who would gather at the blacksmith shop. They loved horses and would judge every one that came in. They knew who had the best horses as well as the drivers. They figured they knew who would take the "Free for All" that year. You could get on their good side by passing around a quart of whiskey. Dave reddened the shoes and pounded them in shape on the anvil with sparks flying in all directions. The horsemen sat on a bench admiring the horse being fitted. It would be a strong contender for the big race, they would encourage the owner. All the compliments would surely cause the owner to pass around the quart of strong drink.

A couple of weeks before the big race Mike and Joe drove Molly to town. A couple of horses were practicing at the site. One of the drivers challenged Joe to a little run to "see if she can catch me," he boasted as he proudly bragged up the speed of his horse. Joe wanted to beat the braggart and leave him away behind but he remembered the strategy he and Mike had made up. Joe was to give the horse her head just to see if she was up to the challenge but then he would hold her back from winning so as not to attract too much notice. Naturally Joe came in a couple of lengths behind so this new horse wasn't seen as a threat.

Dave gave a little whistle of approval as Mike and Joe entered his shop with Molly. "A mighty fine looking mare, Mike," he remarked as a couple of old cronies got up from their bench for a better look. "Give her a nice light set of racing shoes," he told

Dave. My son Joe, here, is going to enter her in the big race. As Dave went about his work he couldn't help but speculate how well she might do. She had good legs and feet and a good muscle tone, he could tell she was in top shape. Mike sat with the old horse fanciers, talking horse, spitting tobacco juice and tipping the bottle every now and then; they predicted that Dr. Morris's horse would take it this year. His driver Al O'Hearn is out at the strip every day exercising. The undertaker has an awful good one too; some say he can beat the doctors. "But that is a mighty fine one you got there, what is her time?" Mike told them he didn't know as they only had a little stretch upriver where Joe runs her.

Molly was lifting her feet high as they left the blacksmith shop. She liked her new shoes, they were so light they felt like slippers and she soon found out that they didn't slip at all as they entered the river ice. She felt like a fast run but Mike cautioned Joe to hold her a little until they got out of sight.

The blacksmith boys stepped outside to see the horse perform. "Look at her go," says one, "he's holding her back," observed another. "She may well be "the dark horse" at the race," cautions another. Before the day was out they learned that Al O'Hearn had tried and beat Mike's horse earlier in the day.

Joe and Mike schemed a plan as they drove Molly homeward. They knew she had a good chance and Mike knew an old horseman who used to win a lot of the races. "If we can get him to coach you on your final preparation it might pay off." A couple of days later Mike and the older gentleman Mr. McLean came to watch and clock Joe run his half mile. Mr. McLean was pleased to be of help and was quick to see what could be improved upon.

"She's fast alright," he offered "but let me see your take off. She is too slow on the start and those town people have been known to play games. If they think someone has a chance to beat their horse, they will encourage their friends to box you in. You have to get off to a jack rabbit start and don't let them box you. Another thing I notice is that your traces are a bit long. If you shorten them up about three links the pung will pull easier and you will have better control. Have you got a gun I can borrow; you have to get used to starting with gunfire from a dead stop. There are sometimes a dozen top horses in the big one, you have to watch both sides and give her a little tap if she needs it."

Mr. MacLean stood at the starting post with a gun in one hand and a stop watch in the other. Joe lined up his horse and when the gun went off he taped Molly on the hip with the whip. The horse took off so fast Joe almost lost his balance, after that there was no need to tap at the start. "Not even O'Hearn can beat that speed," he assured Joe, as he stopped the clock at fifty-five seconds. "Keep practicing" he advised, "But, don't wear her out; let her rest up the day before the race."

The day of the race was a lovely sunny day just a little below freezing. There would be a big turnout by all predictions. Joe gave himself lots of time and arrived around eleven o'clock. The races didn't start until one but he wanted to familiarize his horse to others as he practiced short spurts passing some horses that were also exercising. Whenever he stopped spectators would move in to look over his horse. Most of them would ask her name and give Molly a pat and wish Joe good luck. Others sized her up and down and asked Joe her time but Joe wouldn't give it, and they wondered out loud if she could beat Morris's horse. Mike had pre-registered Joe's horse and he had drawn the number seven. The three judges came over to him and looked over his horse, harness and sleigh. They gave him a large piece of canvas that he was to fasten over the horses back so the number could be easily seen. They did this to all the contenders and at the same time checked, as well as they could, for doping. Some shady characters believed horses would run faster if they were fed a handful of tea. Others gave them a fig of tobacco or a drink of rum. Apparently their thinking is by doping their horse its heart would speed up and therefore run faster but they would be disqualified if found out.

By noon time half the town had turned out. The ice was dotted with black figures on both sides of the half mile strip. Of course there were a lot of horses and sleighs as some families came in from miles around. Everyone was moving around trying to pick the winners. If one wanted to wager a little bit there were a number of bookies mingling around offering two for one odds. If one bet ten dollars, on say number three, they would turn in their marker for twenty dollars if the horse won. Since there were nine horses in the running, the odds were nine to one in favor of the bookies. Everyone wanted to bet a little just for the sport. However, when half the people betting wanted to bet on Morris's horse the bookies stopped taking bets on number five. Mr. O'Hearn had been doing so much bragging about his horse that everyone thought he would take it easily. Since there was no chance to bet on Morris's horse people that could judge horses picked number two, the undertakers horse, or number seven, Joe's horse, because it looked so fit. Of course most people bet on their friend regardless of his chances. It was a way of showing support and should the horse win, they would all rejoice together. Some family members bet against each other, each would pick one horse and whoever's horse was the fastest, regardless how they placed overall, received money from the other as well as bragging rights for the next year.

Excitement was in the air as the first race was run. People were cheering, jumping up and down and clapping their hands as a brown horse and a dapple grey raced along side by side. By the time they reached the finish line the grey was three lengths ahead. Joe moved his horse down along staying out from the crowd but, close enough, so she could see the people and hear the noise. He wanted her to be conditioned to it by the time the big race started. A couple more pair faced off before the other big race. This was a class for horses that never broke the one minute per half mile track. If they did they wouldn't be allowed to compete in this preliminary race.

As advertised the main event was to start at two o'clock with nine of the fastest horses in the country. The two thousand dollar purse was to be divided among the three top entries. There was one thousand for win, six hundred for place and four hundred for show.

Each of the contenders paid a fifty dollar entry fee and the local business council made up the balance to sweeten the pot. In this way only horses that stand a good chance entered.

Everything got awful quiet as the last horse was lined up to the starting line. Joe's heart was beating so loud he was afraid he might not hear the pistol shot. There was a great burst of speed at the start. About six horses were out front at the half way mark. Joe was just cruising along up to this point but he caught O'Hearn taking the lead on his left. There was another one near the inside picking up speed too. It was the undertaker's horse. Joe stayed a little bit behind. At three-quarters it looked like the race was between number five and two. O'Hearn had visions of proudly displaying the cup for the photographers who were set up near the finish line.

As advised by his coach, Mr. MacLean, Joe let the other horse lead, but he kept up close. When he reached the three-quarters mark he was to ask Molly to show her stuff. Joe didn't know if she could do much better but she seemed to be running easy. "Let's go, Molly," he encouraged with a little rattle of the

reins. Molly responded with a little gain every step. By the time
there was only one hundred yards left Molly was a full length
ahead of number two and three lengths ahead of number five. The
red faced, Mr. O'Hearn
was whipping his horse, unmercifully. Joe came in three lengths
ahead of number two and five lengths ahead of number five.

A very happy young man had his picture taken hugging
his horse; another one with the Mayor and council members
presenting the trophy cup. Then he enjoyed the highlight of taking
the winter beauty Queen for a trot up and down through the
spectators. There was great applause as the Queen held up the cup
for everyone to see. Best of all she gave Joe her telephone number
and said she would like to go for a sleigh ride with him again.

While Joe was parading his trophy Mike was calculating
his wagers. He had bet five hundred with a bookie and so he
doubled his money. The bookie said he was glad his horse won,
he would be paying a lot more out if number two had won, as
there were a lot of people betting on the undertaker's horse.

As they were preparing to go home Dr. Morris came over
to shake hands with Joe and Mike. He gave their horse a good
looking over and then he asked Mike if he would consider selling.
"The horse belongs to Joe; you'll have to ask him." Joe was quick
to reply that he would never sell. Dr. Morris said he understood,
but he would like them to think it over. He would like to make
them an offer anyway. He would like to have a winner to add to
his stable. He did most of his racing in summer on tracks all
around the Maritimes. He would be willing to buy Molly for three
thousand and would like to have Joe to come work for him. "Let
me know if you change your mind, young fellow" as he gave him
a little pat on the back.

As they were driving home Mike asked Joe what he
thought of the offer. "Funny what a difference a day, or might I

say a race, can make," he reasoned. "When you drove the horse down on the ice this morning she was worth about five to seven hundred on the market. Look what she is worth now, mostly because you did a good job training her and an excellent job of driving. You know, I picked up a nice little bit of change too because I believed in you."

"Well I know one thing," says Joe, "the time to sell a horse is when they are winning. If I hadn't won Molly would be only worth whatever, like you say, five to seven. We could have lost a lot too. I guess we were lucky this time but it is awful exciting, isn't it?" Joe said he liked working with horses and with that much money he could pick up a couple young horses and train them to be winners also.

"Another option is to take the offer Dr. Morris is giving you. Dr. Morris is a fair man and he has a stable and the connections. If you went with him you could learn a lot just from being around other horsemen at the track. Since you like horses you might want to pursue it as a career and when the time comes start your own stable of fine horses."

"Thanks, Dad, I think I would like just that," says Joe.

March, 2007

TURNING 70

About a week before Christmas we decided to visit our oldest daughter, Paula and David and their three kids, on P.E.I. We went over to take in some highlights of the season. Our two granddaughters, Carrie, aged 12 and Hannah, 11, were playing violins in the school concert. Jared, 13, was instrumental in the design and layout of the programme.

Holidays were just starting so we did some shopping for the kids. The best way to please them, we figured, was to let them pick out something for themselves. All Jared wanted was a couple pair of jeans which he had to try on for fit. We went to several stores in Charlottetown and an afternoon later he had a couple pair that suited.

"Now what would you girls like?" my wife Sylvia asked.

"We have a special store we would like you to take us to," they replied in unison.

"It's right here, park here," they directed me in front of a strip mall.

No big store here, it must be a specialty shop for girls, I thought, as Sylvia and I followed them into a little tack shop. They oohed and aahed as they looked over the inventory. There was a great display of saddles and harness, as well as brushed, combs and horse treats.

Hannah settled for a portable saddle stand. The girls were promised new saddles for Christmas from their parents so she was going to be ready. Carrie settled for new riding boots. Of course they kept saying that they didn't want us spending so much for them. "As long as we have enough left for the bridge," I joked. Sylvia was happy to make the purchases for them as it completed her Christmas shopping.

Only a couple more days and we would be going to Hannah's piano recital at Steel Hall on the U.P.E.I. campus. There were lots of things to do, visit friends and go to hockey games. All three played hockey, as well as their Dad. The new double rink at Pownell was only about two miles from their house and one or the other had a game at different times.

Hannah did us proud at the recital, her continuous practice paid off. She did the best of the fifteen students in her class. I finished the book I was reading, between interruptions and was getting anxious to return home, in spite of Paula's insistence we stay a few more days till Christmas. The roads were in good shape with some snow forecast in the next few days. So we left for home with the assurance that the kids would be over to spend a few days with us before school started up again.

As we were driving home we talked about how the kids were growing up so fast. They seemed to mature so much since we had last seen them in the summer. We wondered if we might live long enough to see what they become. I was thinking that my next birthday would be quite a milestone. I was to reach "the promised land," of three score years and ten on January the 8th. It sure would be nice to get another ten since I am still in good health.

In fact turning seventy really hit me hard, but no one else seemed to notice. Maybe it was self pity, but I couldn't get it off my mind. I was looking forward to having all the family at home sometime before the holidays are over. How many more times; will they all be able to gather with us, I wondered. The younger ones have a great time with Karla and Dean's daughter, who is in second year of nursing at Bathurst.

Every time we talked to them there was something going on at home. I began to wonder if they would make it at all. With only a couple of days left they all descended on us. First the Frasers from P.E.I., then the Marshalls from St. Stephen, complete

170

with Darren's mom and dad who were visiting them. Paula and David decided to sleep at Karla and Dean's house out at the river. However, we all gathered together and ate at our house.

We all had a great time eating and drinking and talking about everything. Whenever the weather was right the boys were out sliding or driving Dean's snowmobile. The girls spent most of the time at the barn with Karla and Jenna's six horses. Whenever they came into the house they were quickly whisked to the basement to change their clothes, as they smelled like horses.

Our house was a beehive of activity for the next two days; People coming and going continually. Sylvia cooking and making dishes as we all ate at our house. There were tractors and trucks all over the floor complete with sound effects. The girls brought their fiddles and they would practice their Christmas carols, jigs and waltzes in the parlor.

Doug, Darren's father, and I were old friends, we were out West together. We talked about things we did and where we had been. Of course we had a continuous supply of wine from my wine cellar. Our biggest job was to keep out of the way with so much going on. As we reminisced I told him I would soon be seventy, Tuesday in fact. He didn't make much fuss over it; he might have asked me how my health was holding up.

Saturday was a very busy day, there seemed to be a lot of traffic between our house and Karla's. About five o'clock "Sylvia announced that were going out for Chinese food and I had better get tidied up. Well, I would have rather stayed home; we had lots of food, besides it would cost a bundle for the whole crowd to eat out. However, there is no sense putting up a fuss and besides I was starting to get hungry.

Reservations were for seven o'clock, I grumbled that it was awful late to be taking kids out. "Quit your complaining and lay off that wine," I was warned. The Frasers were taking their van. Pleadwells were taking their car. Sylvia said she would go with Darren and his mother and I was to follow with Doug in his car. This seemed to be a strange arrangement; I began to suspect there might be a little surprise at the restaurant.

At the town hill Darren made a left turn. Since we were told to follow Doug made a left also. But this is not the way to the restaurant, I reasoned. When he made a turn into the Knights of Columbus hall with all the cars in the parking lot I guessed what was up.

"Too late to turn back now," Sylvia says as they came up to me laughing. What a perfect surprise, the hall was full and all decorated up. Everyone sang out "surprise and Happy Birthday" as I entered in. All my friends were there, I didn't know I had so many, I was overjoyed.

There were about one hundred and twenty-five people; some came a long way. My sisters were over from Fredericton and Sheldon and family came up from Moncton. My cousins from the Nor-west and many local friends; from our own neighbourhood, also. Buddy and Ada said they couldn't make their annual winter trip to Florida till the celebration was over.

I was glad they stayed as Bud brought his guitar and they did some picking and singing. Ken Colepaugh added a lot to the entertainment as he played and sang a song about, "Let me live to see what my kids become as I'm too young to grow old." His other song was dedicated to Sylvia as he sang an old Waylon Jennings tune, "She's a good hearted woman in love with a two timing man. She loves him in spite of the things she don't understand." He got a lot of applause for that one.

Emily brought her keyboard and accompanied the singers. Some friends have told me my granddaughters stole the show with their violin duets.

There was a long table of food set up and everyone helped themselves. Lots of food and drinks, friends and music, made a happy atmosphere. I circulated around the tables and tried to say hello to everyone personally. After that I was placed at the head table facing everyone. My three daughters and Sylvia accompanied me.

Krista was the first to go to the microphone. She said she was waiting ever since her wedding to get even. At her wedding I had made up a poem about her adventures. So she finally got even with a poem about me, some of the good things and some of foolish things also. Everyone had a good laugh.

Not to be outdone, Paula was next to take the mike. She said she admired my writing and read a story I had written about eight years before. The story was about all the advantages of owning a jack-knife. Karla proposed a generous toast, very flattering indeed, as everyone raised their glass to my good health.

With that over I thanked everyone for coming and all the cards and gifts. I told them that over the holidays I was reminiscing about the good times years ago when we used to celebrate with house parties. I was wondering if we could gather enough friends to have one these days. I had forgotten that I had so many friends and turning seventy wasn't so bad after all. Last to be thanked was Sylvia for her part in arranging the surprise with our three daughters. She sure was crafty as she got the local paper and removed the page with the invitation to join us before I read it.

Joyce, Emily and John all had a turn at the mike. They spoke kind words about what a good brother I was. It was a bit exaggerated in my favor I am afraid. Among my friends were three ministers and our member of parliament. The party broke up about ten o'clock with everyone shaking hands and wishing me the best. The women picked up their dishes and cleaned up the hall.

There was a table loaded with gifts and cards. Among

them was a lap-top computer which my girls shared in the expense. We gathered everything up and I would take my time and open the cards and gifts the next day; Sunday morning, after breakfast.

Well, the house was full up with Carrie and Hannah sleeping on an air mattress on the floor in the living room. Upstairs Krista and Darren were in the east room with Doug and Clay in the north room. Cameron and Dylan were in a double bed and Jared in a single in the middle room. Sylvia and I kept our room in the upper room.

About three o'clock Dylan came in to our room. "Grammie there is a chicken under my bed." She took him back and tried to assure him that it was only a dream. They argued back and forth until Cameron woke up and took sides with his brother. I knew that I had to prove to them there was no chicken there, so I went down to the kitchen and got the flashlight. Sylvia held the bedspread up and I, down on my hands and knees shone the light around – no chicken. "Well, it must have went over under Jared's bed," they offered.

We weren't about to draw Jared into this episode as we were all in our underwear. I expected to see their parents walk in on us any minute. The final solution was that I was to stay and sleep with Dylan and Cameron would sleep with Grammie.

The next morning there were some chicken jokes as we ate breakfast together. We hadn't awakened anyone else and no pictures were taken. But we thought it would have made a great one. The picture will remain in my mind for a long time. Things finally got back to normal by Monday, we were alone again as the kids had to return home for school. I had quite a number of thank you cards to send out. Sylvia and I are trying to learn how to run the computer. We have great memories of the party and Doug supplied us with a video disc of pictures of the party to remember it by.

WOMEN'S LIB

I am from the school where men were "King of their Castle." Men, like their peers, did men's work only. They were the bread winners and provided the financial needs of their families. They were respected by their wife and children. Men had the final say and stuck to their guns. Any man, who wasn't in command of his household; lost respect, from his fellow workers. He was looked at as a weakling and was often shunned by real men.

Good women, on the other hand, knew their place. They were proud to be referred to as "so and so's" wife. They were part of his property in all respects. Their role was to please their husbands and have large families. The babies were all breast fed and the older children helped look after their younger siblings. Most women worked from daylight till dark cooking, washing and looking after the children. They often worked late into the night knitting or patching clothes for their man so he would look presentable to his working buddies.

Any physical labor outside the house was considered mans work. They worked hard to ensure they had enough wood and hay for the winter. The older children often helped with the outside chores like feeding the livestock or filling the wood box. There was no need complaining, each did what was expected of them. Men did men's work and women did women's work, everyone was busy and happy.

I have witnessed a great change in just my own generation. Men have lost more in this century then all others. How did this happen, there must have been a women's revolution while I was sleeping. I never noticed it happening, it just crept in. Women are equal to men now in all respects, and making decisions on their own.

I believe the two world wars, especially the second one, were instrumental in women learning more trades. Up till then a few women worked as teachers or nurses. Women supported their men in the first war by knitting wool underwear, socks and mittens. But it was the second war where they really stepped out. They were pressed to work in the factories making all sorts of things to send to the soldiers. They learned to do men's work, they had to, there were no young men left; they were all overseas.

To everyone's surprise they could do the job just as good as the men they replaced. Well, almost anyway, some supervisors even said they were better then men. During this period women learned men's trades like machinists, welders, mechanics, heavy equipment operators and truck drivers.

Ever since, the Second World War, women have been doing men's work. They no longer are referred to as so and so's wife. They have their own name and bow down to no man. They have found ways to control family size, this gives them more free time to do as they please. They have stepped right into mans world and demand equal rights. Men have to be careful what they do or say to their fellow female workers. Some have learned the hard way as they have been accused of assault or sexual harassment.

Not only have women excelled in men's trades, they have become professionals. They are doctors, engineers, lawyers and even air-line pilots. They do pretty well too as I don't hear anyone complaining anymore. Male dominance is nearly a thing of the past. Even the old "men's only" clubs like the Rotary and Elks club have been ordered to open their doors to the women who would like to join. One Rotarian I knew said regretfully that they had to let some women in but they had to bring 'the donuts.' How long before they infiltrate the Free Masons or Knights of Columbus I wonder.

Men have not been so aggressive to enter into trades that

were traditional women's work. I can think of only a few. One
was a male nurse. I never knew there was such a thing twenty
years ago when I entered into the hospital for an operation. It was
less embarrassing having a male shave me in a delicate part of my
body, but I kept a leery eye on him just the same. There were
some rumors that he was gay. I have heard of more men entering
the field lately and they are well received by all. I also know a
man who took maternity leave after his wife had a baby. He did
the same thing when she had their second. He liked it so well he
is now a stay at home dad or a Mr. Mum. She works out earning
more money than he could so they are happy with the
arrangement.

    I used to think a barbershop was a place for men to get a
haircut. My old barber was a good talker, he talked men's stuff
like the news or the economy, and he always had a new off colour
joke. We discussed men going to hair dressers to get their hair
styled. We both agreed that hair dressers were for women and
barber shops were for men. Women barbers just didn't have the
touch, if they put their hand on your head it would feel so light it
would make the chills go up your spine. Well, his partner quit so
guess who was behind the chair the next time I went in. And
guess who didn't flinch when she leaned into my back, and guess
who gave her the two dollar tip.

    I am gradually giving in to women's dominance and I was
spending some time with my daughter and family in St. Sephen.
On Sunday morning I found a great old Presbyterian Church and
went in to worship. Well, the first to greet me was a lady Minister;
she had the robes and collar to show she was a full fledged
minister. I was kind of surprised as back home we didn't
encourage lady ministers. Her sermon, however, was quite
interesting. She didn't talk about the "wrath of God" or "hell fire"
like some likes to do. However, she stressed the great love Jesus

has for us all. I was back a few times and we are on a first name basis now.

I shudder to think what role the male population will play in the next century. If women have come so far in the past few years it is evident they will surpass the male sex anytime. To think they have gained such confidence since they were first allowed to vote in nineteen hundred and twenty-one. Soon we men will be like drone bees.

Who am I kidding, when I think about it a certain woman has dominated my life ever since I said "I do" over forty years ago.

POOR HARRY

"Is that Harry, Harry Williams?' I asked my friend. It looked like him, but I never saw him for some time and he looked like he had fallen on hard times.

"Yes, that's him all right," says Albert as he turns his head so Harry wouldn't see him.

We were at the old car show and it was easy to get lost in the crowd if you wanted to avoid someone. You can also watch someone from a distance without being detected. That is what we did as he brought me up to date on Harry. Harry used to be his friend, or so I thought, by the stories he used to tell. All the fun they were having at the camp site up in the woods.

Albert is my neighbour; he lives only a few houses away. Sometimes when his wife is working the night shift he will come over for a beer. We generally go to the basement to the rec. room for a game of pool. It is also a safe place to talk as Mary can't hear the confidential stories he has for me. They are mostly about the escapades of Harry and his friends up at the camp.

They both have camps up at Loon Lake. There are about a dozen camps in the cluster. They all know each other and visit back and forth on the weekends. They have some great card games, tell stories, get drunk and have some great feeds. Of course they do some fishing, after all that is what they built the camps for.

The camp sites are pretty impressive; some camps look more like a house you might see in town. Most of them are winterized so the owner can go up there every weekend of the year. Of course snowmobiling is a favorite for the winter campers. There is nothing like a big feed and a game of cards after a full day of visiting other camp sites via snowmobile.

Some camp owners bring their wives with them. After a

few weekends of sitting in the camp alone while their husband fishes or helps a camp buddy make some improvement to a camp, they get discouraged and decide to stay home. What is there to get excited about, they wonder. There is nothing to see but trees; No one to see or talk to. The only traffic is the odd half ton or someone bouncing down the trail on a four wheeler. Women don't like to go outside alone up there, too many flies. Not safe, they would complain, a bear or a moose might chase them.

Most camp owners are self sufficient. They have their four wheel drive half ton trucks. They also have a four wheeler, a T.V. on the back just in case the going gets real tough. Of course they have a canoe or two and all the fishing gear that Canadian Tire sells. There is no fishing hole or lake that they can't get to. They know where the moose and deer hang out and are ready when hunting season opens.

The boys are pretty happy up there with no one to bother them. No wife to nag them to go here or there, fix this or that. It is a place to get clear of the stress of the work week. According to Albert they have great fun. Someone or other gets drunk or gets stranded in a mud hole. It takes a whole convoy of comrades to get him out. The next week he might do the same thing all over again. Now that is exciting.

"Now for the confidential stuff," some of the boys have snuck up some strange ladies. One of the campers saw them and told the rest of the guys. Others have thought of that but it was only a fantasy. "Of course if one was to do that the best time would be during the week, all the rest of the group are home working," Albert told me with a nod as he took a drag of beer.

"Now Harry," he kept on; "has been doing that for years. He has his own business and can get away anytime. His wife never goes up to the camp, so he has nothing to worry about. Besides, she is a school teacher and can't get away during the week. He has a couple of different ones he takes up for overnighters. One of the ones, you would know her, if I told you her name. Not a bad looker, at all, you would be surprised, but of course he has the money and they know that. We give him some awful razzings at our Saturday night card games. He is a good sport, he just laughs, an awful nice man though, just like you or I, you would never know he has money."

Every month or so there would come more news about Harry. Sometimes Harry would take another business man up fishing or snowmobiling for a few days. Harry's girl has a friend she takes up for the friend and they make a foursome. He certainly is having a great time, according to Albert. "Of course, he has the money," he always adds.

"Harry is not a young man," I remind him, "he is probably older than I. You would think he would be satisfied with one woman."

"Yes, but a little strange stuff never hurt anyone," Albert says with a laugh.

"He has a lot to lose if he gets caught. I have seen his wife a few times, she is a very nice looking woman, quite a bit younger than he, I suspect."

"Yes, I know," says Albert, 'but he says she doesn't like the woods and won't go up with him at all. She is kind of high society, belongs to all kinds of theatre and cultural associations. She does a lot of volunteer work, things like that. I guess she goes her way and he goes his."

About a year ago I was surprised to see in the paper that Harry had sold his business. Kind of young to retire, I thought, he will have more time for the camp now. I mentioned this to my friend Albert and was surprised by his reaction.

"He had to sell it, he needs the money; he is getting a divorce. His wife caught him, you know."

"Oh, I didn't know."

"Yes, some sort of emergency came up a couple of months now. Oh yeah, I remember, his old mother was in the old age home and she was on her death bed. They tried to reach him but his cell phone was off. It was getting late so his wife got her sister to drive up to the camp with her. I guess they walked right in on him and the one in bed together, the rest is history, so to speak."

"He had to sell the business and divide the money. She got to keep the house and he has the camp. Of course the camp is as good as any house but it is not worth that much due to the remote location. Anyway, his family is all put out at him and his children won't even speak to him. That is not right, I think, after all he gave them anything they wanted."

We watched Harry follow a few steps behind a young copper toned lady. She was probably in her forties but dressed much younger in a pair of cut-off jean shorts and a halter top. She didn't look too bad from a distance in her short shorts and her tan and blonde hair.

"Is she the one he is living with?" I asked Albert.

"Yes, that is the young tramp, she sure made a fool out of him," he grumbled. "Just after his money, that was all. He is practically broke now; they live most of the time up at his camp. I guess she keeps a small apartment on Gordon Street, they stayed there last winter. Neither of them are working, I don't know how they live. He was over to a party the other weekend and kept complaining that his wife took him to the cleaners. His truck is pretty well worn out and he can't afford to trade. We all feel sorry for him and take up extra groceries which we leave behind for him when we go out."

Everyone is getting tired of helping him out and listening to his hard luck story. It is time they found a job. There must be something he can do. She could get a job somewhere, a waitress or something like that, but he doesn't want to let her out of his sight.

"Oh well," I said, "when you have something everyone else wants you hate to lose it."

"Yes but it is a luxury he can't afford. One can live cheaper than two, right. I don't know who would want her anyway, after the way she took Harry."

"No, I suppose," I said as we walked away. But, I thought, you did a few years before. There was no one as smart or lucky as Harry. You would have done the same thing if you had the chance.

AN UNEVENTFUL EVENT

I was looking forward to the weekend, having survived a weekend of working in the cold damp weather. After all, it was the first week of June and the weatherman was calling for two days in a row of warm sunny weather. My plan was to meet up with some friends in town to go up to the annual prospector's field trip in the Bathurst area. Then if I could get back early enough there might be time to plant some garden.

We knew Karla's horse was going to foal sometime soon. She was so excited Aztec was finally going to have an offspring. That is quite a story by itself, you see, she had been waiting for two years. About two years ago they decided it would be nice to get a foal. She was sixteen and horses only live to see their twenties as a rule. Aztec is a beautiful horse and she had paid a lot of money for her. She wanted the perfect stallion for her; he had to be good looking with a good temperament.

The search was on; she inquired among her horse friends where to look. One weekend it was to Moncton, they saw some nice ones but couldn't quite make up their minds. Another time they went to Sackville, still not quite what she had in mind. There was one more place she wanted to see. There was this horse trainer by the name of Stewart App who lived near Sussex, and his stallion was highly recommended.

Stewart's stallion met and exceeded all qualifications. The horse was shiny and muscular. He was tall and kind; he would obey his master's voice command, what a horse! They were sold after they looked at some foals he had sired that were still in the barn. The price was quite high, more than the other breeders were asking, but Stewart knew he had a superior horse. They came to an agreement that they would send Aztec down. Stewart recommended that they should leave her there for a month to make sure she was bred. After all, it was quite a distance to trailer a horse. Even though, he guaranteed a free breeding if she didn't have a live foal. Their chances would be better; they would save on the trucking.

Karla and Dean were so impressed with the stallion that they decided they would send Whitney, their other mare, down to Stewart's also. The trucking wouldn't cost any more for two than for one as the truck had to make the trip anyway. They made arrangements for Danny Foran, a local livestock dealer, to make the delivery for them.

He arrived on a Saturday morning in the spring of 2002. Karla had to work that day and Dean was busy farming. I volunteered to go along to make sure the horses landed safely. Danny might need some help loading and unloading. Besides, I wanted to see this wonderful stallion myself. There was a young bull in the thirty foot trailer; he was on his way to a farm in Plaster Rock. We unloaded him and put the two horses loose in the front half of the trailer. We wouldn't have to shift them again until we got to Stewarts.

Danny was a typical trader and we delivered the young bull with all his papers of pedigree to a large dairy farm. The farmer was pleased with his purchase of this new bull that came off a dairy farm in P.E.I. Next we loaded his large bull on the back of the trailer to a farmer in Keswick Ridge. Danny made arrangements to pick up a couple of his cull cows the next time he passes by. Along the way to Stewarts Danny stopped in at another farm and purchased a large cow that had outlived her usefulness. She would be shipped to Quebec along with a half dozen others that he had back home, he told me.

Stewart told me that we had two fine horses. He especially liked Aztec and said the two of them should make a beautiful baby. He would take good care of them and call when they are ready to come home. Danny and I admired his stallion and beautiful facilities and headed for home. A couple more stops before we landed back on the Miramichi, with an old dairy cow, a beef cow and an old work horse that was about thirty years old. He had to promise the old man he bought him from that he would be going direct to the canners. The old gentleman thought that would be more humane than to sell him to someone who might make him work hard or abuse him.

A couple of months later Danny dropped off Karla's mares. Stewart told them he was sure Whitney was bred but he wasn't so sure about Aztec. Anyway, they could send her back next year if she didn't catch. There was medicine available that they could give her before bringing her back if necessary. Sure enough, last spring Whitney delivered a beautiful large foal, but Aztec had to make a return trip to Stewart App's. She returned a couple of months later but Stewart said he didn't think she conceived, perhaps she had some physical problem or was too old.

Karla was saddened but kept caring and riding Aztec as Whitney was out of commission with a young filly for a while. Sometime this spring she noticed Aztec was getting thin. At the same time she was putting on a hay gut. Perhaps it was old age starting to show or it could be bad teeth. She may need to have her teeth floated so she can eat better. When she started to bag up Karla asked herself – could the horse be pregnant after all. It was soon obvious she was right, she was elated and so began feeding more and foal ration to help condition her for the event.

Just as I was about to go to bed Friday night Karla's daughter Jenna tore into the house all out of breath. "Aztec is starting to give birth." "Get your coat and boots on." Sylvia commanded. "They may need some help." As I entered the barn I was shushed to be very quiet. There was the mare lying down in the maternity ward. It was a large stall with about six inches of shavings on the floor. There was also hay and water for the horse. Just outside the stall there was warm water, long surgical gloves and a box of clean rags, just in case. Lawn chairs were set up and there was a silent audience. Two of our horse loving neighbours, Liz and Kathy, were seated and gave me a nod as I entered.

Karla was at the mare's head stroking her neck and talking gently to her. Dean was at the other end with long plastic gloves on. He had a hold of the colt's front feet which were exposed, but still in the sac. He would give a little tug every time the horse had contractions. "Make sure the head is in between the legs," I warned him. After a few more minutes the head started to appear. The mare tossed and rolled back and forth for quite some time. It was a very large colt. "Pull harder," I encouraged and jumped in to help them. A few more contractions and pulls and out popped the foal with a big splat. Break the sac so it can breathe and wipe the mucus from its mouth, was the first thing to do. The foal gave a big stumble and we were all relieved, it was alive.

The mare was spent, she gave a glance back and then stretched her neck on the fluffy shavings to catch her breath. After ten minutes it became obvious to us that the mare was still in distress. She was rolling from one side to the other and was straining to pass the afterbirth, but it wouldn't come.

"Call Krista," she is our veterinarian daughter who lives in Alberta.

"No, call Sue, we need a vet here right fast," says Dean.

Luckily we have a telephone in the barn, Jenna made the call.

"Leave a message and I'll get back to you as soon as possible." Not much consolation when you are in a jam.

"Call Krista then," after all Krista knew Aztec was expecting.

"What can we do?" Jenna asked.

"First tell me, what, is she acting like," Krista asks.

"She's in a lot of pain."

"How's her pulse, it should be around forty. Has she got a temperature?" Krista questioned.

It was kind of confusing to say the least, some were passing on information, others checking this and that and some of us asking stupid questions, everyone was trying to help.

"How is the foal?" Krista asked.

"Oh, he is a perfect little lad, well not so little, he is so tall, he stands even with my belt," I offered.

"Has he had a suck yet?" she asked.

"No, the mare is so bothered she won't have anything to do with him."

"You will have to milk her, put the milk in a bottle and feed him, it is paramount he gets the mares milk with colostrums in it. Milk her and keep some ahead, you may be glad if anything should happen to the mare. We managed to get some milk into a cup from the downed mare. Then it was straight to the foal that licked his lips in approval.

While talking to Krista Sylvia heard a beep. "Call back later," she told her daughter, and took the call. It was Sue, our local vet; she said she would be right up.

The foal was born at 10:45 and this was one hour later. One has to be dedicated to do that job. By the time she arrived; the mare seemed more content to die than live. Sue was quick with a couple of needles. She went to work examining the horse; she found a lot of damage internally and was afraid of infection setting in.

By two-thirty the horse was up on her feet and seemed to be more comfortable. The colt was all dried off and looked more beautiful than ever, he was a solid chocolate colour. I said good-night to the ladies, who were going to stand vigil all night. After all, I still might be able to get a little sleep and go to Douglastown

Tim Horton's for seven in the morning to meet up with my prospecting buddies.

At 6 am I checked with the girls. The horse was a little better, I was relieved. I made it on time and we had a lovely day in the Bathurst area. Everything was O.K. at the barn when I returned. We managed to plant some garden before the horse race started. The Belmont was being run at eight o'clock. It was the crown jewel of the three most famous races. "Smarty Jones," won the Kentucky Derby then the two year old won the "Preakness" two weeks later, leading by seven lengths. There were nine horses in this third race and it was twenty-seven years since a horse won the Triple Crown. Everyone thought Smarty Jones would walk away with it this time. The commentators were guessing which horse might come second since Jones was in a class of his own. There was a five million dollar bonus for any horse to win all three.

We were on the edge of our seat as another horse poked his nose by Smarty at the finish line. I felt sorry for the owner; he was seventy-eight years old and was being wheeled in a wheelchair as he inhaled oxygen through a plastic tube in his nose. Later that evening Toronto Blue Jays lost the game after a winning streak. The Calgary Flames lost the hockey game to Tampa Bay. Well, maybe tomorrow will be better; it is supposed to be sunny.

Karla stayed with her horse till five in the morning then went home. When Jenna checked on them in the morning, we were enjoying our typical Sunday breakfast of blueberry pancakes and sausage. I heard her coming up from the barn screaming. The horse must be down, I thought.

I ran to see what, was the matter.

"The foal is dead," she blurted.

"What happened?" She didn't know. At first she thought

he was just sleeping in his own little pen just off from the mares pen.

It was the same solemn crowd at the barn again as Sue came to have a look at the colt and also to check on the mare.

I guess an autopsy wouldn't prove anything now. Without one there was no way of telling, she explained. Sometimes things just happen for no reason. Sort of like a crib death of a perfectly healthy baby.

"Better in the barn than in the house; my mother always said" says Sylvia and we all agreed.

After that Dean got his friend Harry to come with his backhoe. There were some wet eyes as the little lad was buried between the apple trees in the bottom of the orchard.
He is not alone, several horses, dogs and ponies are resting in the same area. We have fond memories of them but don't mark the individual graves, sometimes we would like to forget.

Jenna's mare is due to foal in a couple of weeks. The Vet says she may have twins by the size of her. However, that is something I am not looking forward to. I might add that Aztec seems to be improving every day.

www.ingramcontent.com/pod-product-compliance
Lightning Source LLC
Chambersburg PA
CBHW061206170626
46809CB00003B/1261